The Cinder Earl's Christmas Deception

Contrary Fairy Tales: Book 2

Em Taylor

Copyright

Cover Art: Rebeca Ira-P

Dedication

This book is dedicated to the ladies who have helped the book come to fruition. To Suzie and Jo who kept me writing it. To Michelle, Joanne and Lindsay who checked for inconsistencies, grammar mistakes and spelling errors. To Vero who made so many changes to the cover it's not funny. She must be cross eyed by now. And to anyone who has believed in me the many, many times my own faith in myself has wavered. Thank you all.

Chapter 1

December 4th, 1816

"Have you finished polishing Mr Cedric's Hessians, My Lord?" asked Cochrane, the valet of Gabriel Marchby's half-brother. Gabriel pointed to the gleaming boots sitting near the fire and admired his own work. Even Cedric couldn't complain about the shine he had achieved on the fashionable boots.

Gabriel tossed the shirt he was mending on the large table in the servants' hall and sat back, stretching his arms and legs. What would the _grande dames_ of the _Ton_ think if they knew the eldest son of the Duke of Hartsmere sat below stairs mending his bastard half-brother's clothes, instead of living in the country 'because of his poor health' as they had been told?

Cochrane picked up the boots just as Annie, one of the scullery maids, came hurrying into the room and over to the large dresser. She picked up a serving salver and flashed Gabriel a 'come hither' smile.

It was tempting, he had to admit. Annie was voluptuous—big-breasted, broad-hipped, pouty-lipped, and the lock of blonde hair escaping from her white cap was somewhat arousing to a man who had been without for some months. But, while aesthetically she was pleasing, she was not his usual fare in muslin. He did not make a mess on his own doorstep—he did not bed the maids. He bedded the gentry. They knew how to keep their mouths shut.

Governesses were best. They may not plan to marry but they did not want anyone one to know they no longer possessed their virtue. And he was seldom the man to take it.

But they were willing, pliant, intelligent, and excellent students in the bedchamber. And on occasion, in his younger years, it had been he who had been the student. Of course, doubted that one could call his small servant quarters a bedchamber.

So Annie was out of the question. He would have to wait until he could find a woman who was up to his higher standard. More befitting the legitimate heir of a duke.

The maid bustled out and Cochrane sat down on the chair next to Gabriel.

"Do you fancy a night in the Boar's Head? You have the night off and Thomson and I plan to get drunk. We might pick up a couple of tarts. You never know your luck."

Gabriel studied the valet. "What time do you need to get home for Cedric?"

"He won't be home until three at least. It's the Haringey ball."

"Oh, he shall be out carousing after that. He may not even need you. He may bring home his own tart."

"I had better be prepared to have the whole room treated for lice, fleas and God knows what all. I can feel myself scratching at the very thought. Where does he dig these creatures up from? I swear the tarts that us mere paupers bed are much cleaner than the things he brings home."

"You know it's possible he's the one with fleas and the French pox, rather than the tarts," suggested Gabriel, unable to hide the wicked gleam in his eye. Cochrane's mouth twisted as he attempted not to smile.

"I am sure I have no idea what you mean, My Lord."

"Stop calling me 'My Lord.' I'm as much a servant here as you, and always have been."

"You are the Earl of Cindermaine and heir to the Duke of Hartsmere. You are and always will be a lord to us, *My Lord*."

Gabriel sighed. "As you wish."

"How many times have we had this discussion?" asked the valet, as Gabriel picked back up Cedric's shirt.

"Far too many."

"Indeed. It's time to put things right."

"I do not want to hear this."

"You're a stubborn bastard."

"As I recall, the problem is that I am the one who is not a bastard."

"Indeed, you are not, My Lord. There are many things you are not, and it is time you knew and accepted those too."

"Bugger off and get on with your work, Cochrane."

Cochrane tugged his forelock and bowed low; the sarcasm evident from his gesture. Gabriel found the rip he was mending and began to sew, ignoring the muttered curse from his departing friend.

Chapter 2

"He is the illegitimate son of a duke," Miss Kathleen Roberts grumbled as she strolled through Hyde Park with her sister on the fourth day of December 1816. "Mr Cedric Onslow." She thought the name over and over in her head a few times.

"Onslow is not a terrible name. No worse than Roberts," pronounced her sister.

"His father acknowledges him and his brother, but honestly Teresa—an illegitimate son. Alas, Papa tells me it is necessary for the business, and I must do my duty. I suppose I always knew it would come to this—an arranged marriage. I had hoped to become a viscountess at the very least, rather than a mere Mrs." She huddled into the fur collar of her winter pelisse, trying to ignore the blustery wind and the sleet.

It was not the best weather for a walk in the park, but she had wanted to get out of the house before she had said anything to her parents she may have regretted.

"Mama has no title, and she is perfectly content," replied her younger sister, looking equally cold and throwing a longing glance back at the barouche which sat on the carriage drive next to Rotten Row just a short distance away.

Hyde Park was quiet that afternoon. A couple of nannies walked along the grass with small children. A few men on horseback rode along on elegant mounts, chatting and chuckling heartily, and a few young bucks came charging up Rotten Row on their snorting brown steeds calling out challenges to one another.

Kathleen considered her sister's words and turned from the race she was watching. "But she married Papa for love. I do not have that luxury."

"Indeed. But perhaps he will be handsome and charming and have a scintillating personality."

"Perhaps. I can but hope."

"Do not be downhearted, Kathleen. Oftentimes love grows between a man and a woman when they must marry for the sake of their families. Mr Onslow might be exactly what your heart desires, even if he does not seem it at first glance. And you shall meet him tomorrow."

"Yes, and then our betrothal ball is the next evening. It is all rather rushed. But I suppose Mama wishes to return to America as soon as possible, so she wishes to see me settled and happy."

"Indeed. She would like to return in time for the birth of Patrick's baby. Oh, I cannot wait to be an aunt. Then it shall be your turn and I shall be an aunt twice over."

Kathleen smiled at her sister who was just eighteen years old. She would be allowed to be part of the entertainments this Christmas Season before being whisked away, back to America and the long six-week voyage to get there.

Teresa would enjoy the delights of the *Ton* and all its lavish entertainments, of that, Kathleen had no doubt. And young men aplenty would solicit her hand for a dance or a stroll. She hoped her flighty younger sister would not have her head turned too easily. And she would hopefully be back next year for her own entry into society.

"Perhaps I have been too harsh on Papa. After all, how awful could this gentleman be?"

"Quite. Therefore, now you have convinced yourself that you are not destined for a life of marriage to a fairy tale ogre, please can we return to the carriage? I believe my feet have turned to ice and I have ruined my half-boots with this wet grass." Teresa's voice had a whiny quality to it and frankly, while she had a little more optimism about her future, Kathleen still could not help feeling uneasy about this arranged marriage. She did not like it one bit. But she held back her misgivings and smiled sunnily at her sister.

"Fine. Let us go home and get a warm cup of chocolate to heat us through. I cannot wait to read more of Sense and Sensibility."

"Don't you just love Edward Ferrars?" asked Teresa.

"Edward?" asked Kathleen, raising an eyebrow. "Surely you mean Colonel Brandon."

"Brandon? But he's old."

"Hmm," Kathleen replied. "Come, my little Marianne, let us get you home before you catch a fever, and some weak-willed dandy sweeps you off your feet."

"Pardon?"

"Nothing."

∞   ∞   ∞

Cochrane's words still rang in Gabriel's ears. He'd felt distracted all day. Whistling, he hurried down the street on his way home from the subscription library, an errand he had run for his twin sister, Christina. The sweet girl often used his services for less taxing jobs, knowing it would mean his sire would not make him do dirty and physically demanding tasks. The Duke treated Christina as a family member, not a servant. But then she had not done what Gabriel had done when they were five years old. Christina was not a bad person. Not like him. He shook the thought aside. He didn't usually dwell on the past—on what he had done. There was no point.

He needed to pay attention, especially on the streets of Mayfair. He should be looking out for people who may still recognise him from Eton and Oxford.

Because Gabriel would inherit the Ducal title and estates in the event of his sire's death, the Duke had felt it his duty to send Gabriel to the best school and university money could afford, even if he cared nought for his legitimate heir. And so, Gabriel had worked as a servant in the holidays and gone to school and university like a normal Duke's heir in term time. Now the Duke treated Gabriel as a servant all the time.

But in town, most people did not see beyond his cap and servants clothing. It was a simple disguise and usually effective.

"Cindermaine?" The man who had called out his name was almost past him. Gabriel lowered his head and continued walking, but a wooden cane blocked his path at chest height. "Cindermaine, it is you?"

Affecting an East London accent, Gabriel tried to push past the barrier.

"Sorry Guv'nor. You got the wrong bloke."

A chuckle then, "Oh no. I'd know you anywhere, Gabriel."

Myles, Viscount Stalwood, his best friend from Eton and then Oxford, took a step back and bent down to peek under his cap.

"I don't fink so, milord. Please let me by."

He pushed hard and the cane gave way but Stalwood was upon him. The viscount had him by the scruff of the neck and was holding his cane to his throat as though it was a sword. Gabriel realised it probably had a damned sword inside. He winced as he recognised that while his street brawling skills may be top notch, his upper-class fighting and fencing skills needed polishing.

"Say what, did this ruffian try to rob you, old chap?" asked a well-heeled, well-meaning passer-by. "Shall I get the Bow Street Runners?"

"Oh, no need for that. He's one of my servants who ran away. Got the kitchen maid in an interesting condition. Just going to make sure he does the right thing," said Stalwood, glee dripping in his tone.

"Ah, quite right. Quite right. Too many poor young girls left carrying the baby. Make him face his responsibilities." The passer-by gave Gabriel a prod in the belly with his own cane as he walked off. Gabriel winced. He was grateful though. He suspected the passer-by had been aiming for his groin. Thank heavens the old man was a dreadful shot.

"You can let me go now." Gabriel growled.

"Will you try to run away?" asked Stalwood.

"No."

"Nice to see you have retained your accent after all."

"Bugger off."

"It's lovely to make your acquaintance too after all this time, friend."

Gabriel scowled as he straightened his clothing.

"I refer you to my previous statement."

"We need to talk," said Stalwood.

"No, Stalwood. We do not. I need to go home. Goodbye."

"Cindermaine, if you move, I will yell that you have robbed me. You shall be in Newgate within half an hour. Dressed as you are, we both know, I have the advantage here."

Gabriel sighed and turned back to his former friend. Then he bobbed a servant's bow. "My sister will cover my absence from my duties if you can think of a suitable place where we might talk, My Lord."

"My townhouse is just around the corner. We may as well go there."

"As you wish, *My Lord.*"

They walked in silence to Curzon Street, then Stalwood took him in through the front door. Gabriel who had been attempting to walk a step behind Stalwood all the way to his townhouse arched an eyebrow at this sign of equality.

"At least enter ahead of me, My Lord," Gabriel muttered. "I am after all a commoner, being an earl only by courtesy. While you are a viscount and thus, a peer of the realm."

Stalwood glowered but walked ahead of Gabriel, giving his hat, gloves and great coat to the butler and waiting for Gabriel to give his cap to the butler. The butler, to his credit, did not show his distaste for his master's company.

"Tea and brandy, Campbell. In the library."

"As you wish, My Lord." The butler bowed and moved off and Stalwood led the way to the library. Gabriel could not help feeling like he was back at Eton and heading to the master's study for punishment. He could almost hear the Greek declensions rattling around in his brain.

"So, you dress like a servant, yet I've seen your father, your sister and your half-brothers around town. Your family are not paupers. What the devil is going on, Cindermaine?"

"Pour the brandy and give me some paper, ink and a pen so I may send a note to my sister, that she may know what has happened to me and cover for me."

Stalwood pointed to the desk where the requested items lay and headed for the decanter. Gabriel scrawled a quick note to his sister and Stalwood arranged for a messenger to take it directly to Lady Christina Marchby.

When Stalwood returned to the library, Gabriel regarded him sullenly as he swirled the amber liquid around. It was nice to sit at a proper hearth in a real library opposite his friend the way he was supposed to do. Stalwood had asked a question.

"I did something many years ago, and this is my penance. When my father dies and I inherit the title, he cannot stop me living the life I was born to lead, but until then, he holds the purse strings. If I want to eat, I work for a living."

"What did you do?"

"I refuse to discuss it."

"Was this before or after university?"

Gabriel hesitated. "Before."

"So, you were a boy."

"Yes."

"Before or after school."

"Before."

"You were in leading strings?"

"Not quite but I was young, yes. But I knew right from wrong." Gabriel watched the fire, unable to bear, the disappointment in his old friend's face.

"Why do you work for your father if you have no money? You have an excellent education. You could work in a career that the gentry would hold—a doctor, a solicitor, a man of business."

"I am the spitting image of my father and one of my half-brothers. Someone would recognise me. It would be a scandal. I am protected as a servant in my father's household. More importantly, this way my twin sister is protected from the scandal. She must marry eventually, though she shows no sign of settling down yet. Besides, I owe my father. It was he and my mother whom I wronged."

"Your mother died when you were, what? Five? Did she not? Were you responsible?"

"I said I did not want to discuss it." Gabriel drained his brandy in two gulps. The burn as the expensive spirit rushed down his gullet soothed his frayed nerves.

Meeting Myles Stalwood again after all this time had set him back on his heels. He had left that part of his life behind him—a time when despite the cloud of his mother's death and the darkness of his home life, he'd been carefree and happy. Eton and Oxford had been wonderful. He'd had many friends, but Myles had been the best. They had got into so much trouble together, dreamed great dreams of joining the army together, though, as heirs apparent to their respective titles and estates, that could never be.

But that was a long time ago and now Stalwood was prying into things that did not concern him.

"Well, it has been lovely to catch up, but I must be off, Stalwood. Thank you for the brandy."

"Oh no. We are not done yet. What are you going to do?"

"Well, I thought I'd go to White's, read the papers, have dinner, and then go to the Haringay's ball. Then perhaps a gaming hell or three," replied Gabriel, sarcasm dripping off every word. "You?"

Stalwood's gaze narrowed. "I thought I might punch you in the face until your attitude changed, then I may get some sense out of you. I like my idea better."

"But if I hit back, your poor butler would find you on your arse with a broken nose, a broken jaw and crushed ballocks when I had accidentally stepped on them on my way out."

"You and whose army, Cindermaine," chuckled Stalwood derisively.

Gabriel opened his mouth to reply with a witty rejoinder when a knock sounded at the door. Campbell, the butler, entered holding a small silver salver with a note on it. He held it out to Stalwood, who took the note, read it, and thanked the butler.

"Show her in, Campbell. Looks like your cavalry has arrived, Cindermaine."

Stalwood rose to his feet and Gabriel did likewise. His eyebrows practically flew into his hairline when Christina, a vision in a dark pink pelisse with fur collar and matching bonnet strode into the library.

She halted a proper distance from their host and curtseyed.

"Lord Stalwood."

"Lady Christina."

"Oh, no need to introduce us, Gabriel. It really is fine. Just stand there gaping," said his sister waving a gloved hand at him.

Gabriel frowned.

"I believe neither of you gave me the opportunity to introduce you. Lord Stalwood, this is my older sister, Lady Christina. Christina, this is Viscount Stalwood. We used to be friends at school and university."

It was the turn of Stalwood and Christina to scowl.

"I am precisely eight minutes older than this brute," Christina said.

"I know. He used to complain about you lording it over him."

"He did?" Christina's smile was radiant with this news.

"Yes. He says I am a former friend, but I am happy to be his friend on a continuing basis if he will stop being a proud idiot for a few minutes and allow me to be so. I do not care if he is forced to work like a servant. He is still Gabriel Marchby, Earl of Cindermaine."

"Indeed he is. I wish you had found him sooner." There was a slight sigh at the end of Christina's words

"Alas, I have not been in town. I went to the country when I married."

"So, do you plan to go back?" Christina's brow had creased and her eyes shone with disappointment. Gabriel wondered if she'd been hoping that Stalwood would somehow help him. He wanted to roll his eyes. Silly, wonderful, endearing girl.

"No. I stayed so long because my wife ... well, she died in childbed giving birth to our son Henry. I have been out of half-mourning for over a year. My parents and Charlotte's parents are in town, so I thought I should come up with Henry for the Christmas Season. Time to start living again. Charlotte would have wanted that."

"I am so terribly sorry. Were you very much in love?"

"Christina!" barked Gabriel. "I am sorry, Stalwood. Bloody stupid and prying question to ask. You have been reading too many romance novels. Read books that will broaden your mind."

Stalwood chuckled. "Actually, no. Not very much. I liked her a lot and we dealt extremely well together. We held each other in very high esteem and were becoming good friends. I missed her terribly when she died. But love? No. Ours was an arranged marriage. But do not for one moment think I did not care or that I do not care, even now."

"I understand. Thank you for telling me and I do apologise for prying."

"Well, you are the sister of a very dear friend even if he is being a prize idiot at present. Now, take a seat and we shall have tea. Then we shall arrange another afternoon like this so we might at least all get to know one another properly, and Cindermaine can have some time off."

The next hour passed pleasantly. No more was said about the reasons for Gabriel's work as a servant nor of the events that had led to it. Stalwood led the conversation, telling tales of their time at Eton, while Christina filled in some stories of their childhood, first at Marchby Castle, a day's carriage ride outside of London and then at Hartsmere Estate in Yorkshire.

When it was time to leave, Stalwood did not push things. He simply said he would see Gabriel on Tuesday and wished him well. The men had an understanding. Gabriel ignored the brightness shining in his sister's eyes as they walked to her carriage and he climbed atop to sit with the driver.

Chapter 3

Kathleen did not know where to look. His eyes. Concentrate on his eyes. They were brown. She usually liked brown eyes. Mr Cedric Onslow's eyes were a bit ... well ... hard, sneering, unkind. It was difficult to express, but she was not sure she liked them. But she had to give him the benefit of the doubt and trust her papa.

Mr Onslow was waiting for her to sit before he moved to his seat. This was not good. If she sat, her eyes would be level with the most revealing part of his inexpressibles.

"Please, Mr Onslow, will you not have a seat? The tea trolley will be here in just a moment."

"Ah yes. Thank you, my dear. I don't mind if I do." He marched over to an armchair and sat down, his legs splayed. Kathleen swallowed hard.

Well, she supposed she would have to get used to that part of his anatomy if she had to marry him.

He was most definitely a dandy. The style of his cravat knot was over the top and fussy—as if his valet had spent hours getting it just right. His frilly cuffs were completely impractical and must get in the way constantly, his garish waistcoat would give anyone a headache, and his skin-tight inexpressibles—a form of menswear that few men would contemplate due to the fact they left absolutely nothing to the imagination, horrified her. In fact, she could even see the outline of ... *it* ... through the fabric.

She had not seen inexpressibles before coming to England. They just did not exist in New Hampshire. It seemed the gentlemen in America were less fashionable, which she could not help but think was a good thing. Unwed young ladies should not know about that part ... or those parts of a man's anatomy. She had seen them on statues in the museum but in real life ...? She shuddered.

Even the tassels on his shining Hessians were too big, gaudy and showy. She was trying very hard not to judge him on his clothing alone, but it was very difficult.

Kathleen's mother poured tea for everyone, and Kathleen handed around the cups. The Duke of Hartsmere grunted something that may have been a thank you, but she could not be sure. He looked very severe, and very like his son, though he wore much more conservative clothing.

Her own father was his usual jovial self, keeping conversation to discussing the weather and the upcoming entertainments of the Christmas Season. Teresa sat demurely, all rather overawed by the thought of a real duke being in the same room as her lowly American family. And Mr Onslow's brother, Godfrey, another dandy, sat with a disaffected air, inspecting his fingernails and looking utterly bored with the whole affair.

Kathleen's gaze caught that of her mother's as she returned to the chaise she was to share with her.

What was that she saw in Mama's gaze? Understanding, caring? Please God, let it not be pity. An unwanted chill crept up Kathleen's spine. Elizabeth Roberts pitied her own daughter.

Kathleen swallowed hard and raised her chin. She was no weakling and had weathered bigger storms than this. She could take this dandy in hand. Surely he was a decent fellow underneath. She sat down and accepted the cup from her mama.

"So, our betrothal ball tomorrow shall be in Hartsmere House. My mother is organising it, although obviously, given the scandal ..." Cedric stopped for a moment to cough ... and cough. His face went bright red as he grabbed his handkerchief from his pocket to cough into it. "I do apologise," he croaked after a moment and a gulp of tea. "I believe the wet, windy weather may have affected me. Where was I. Ah yes, my mother is organising it but unfortunately cannot be the hostess, as you must be aware. She married the late Baron Benwick after my brother and I were born and although we could not take his name as my father had already accepted us as his own, she is still the Dowager Baroness. Much though the *Ton* accepts my parents ... ah ... arrangement in private, so to speak, in public, they could not possibly host a ball together."

"Oh for God's sake, do stop twittering Cedric." The Duke's voice was a low growl, as he looked first at his son then at Kathleen's papa. "Truth is, Portia knows her way around a ballroom and decorations. The place will look just as expected. Good grief man, have you got the ague?" He had turned to Cedric who had turned the colour of beetroot as he had succumbed to another bout of coughing. Once the poor man had stopped almost retching, he hauled in a breath and turned sheepishly to address his overbearing father.

"I ... err, I have to admit, I do not feel to be in particularly good health. I feel a little light-headed."

His father let out a weary sigh.

"All right. Well, suffice it to say that everything is in order for tomorrow night. We shall have a family meal at eight. The ball shall start at eleven. The Dowager Baroness will be in attendance, but she will accompany Godfrey. I shall be the host along with my sister, Lady Eleanor Stanbury. Right, I had better get Cedric home, so he is well for tomorrow. Come, boy."

Cedric stood on distinctly shaky legs. He was looking rather green now. The Duke bowed over the ladies' hands, as did Godfrey. Cedric merely nodded his head to them as he coughed into his handkerchief. His brother whacked him on the back a few times, a look of distaste on his face, causing his lip to curl comically.

Kathleen's papa walked them out to the door. Kathleen, Teresa and their mama stood back from the bay window, just enough in the shadow so that no one on the street would see them gawping at the men as they left. The Duke strode with purpose and elegance towards the large carriage.

A liveried footman held open the door for his master. A coachman sat atop the box keeping the four perfectly matched blacks steady. The four horses were beautiful, and it was obvious that the Duke took great pride in them.

Godfrey helped his brother out of the house and onto the street. Just before they got to the carriage, however, Cedric reached out his hand

and grabbed the shoulder of the footman. The footman lurched out of the way as Cedric used his other hand to grab the edge of the carriage.

Kathleen covered her eyes and groaned. The poor man. Her mama yelped and turned away from the window and Teresa cried out before stating the glaringly obvious.

"Cedric just cast up his accounts all over the side of the carriage. I think he hit the back of the horse and the poor footman too. Uh! The poor horse."

"Poor Cedric," said Kathleen, feeling the need to defend her betrothed. The man was clearly unwell.

"Poor footman," commented her mother, moving over to ring the bell to have the tea tray taken away. "Now, what do you think of Cedric?"

Kathleen had to admit that on first impressions, she had not liked him. He had seemed a little ridiculous and unable to think before he spoke. But she had not spoken properly to him.

"I barely had a chance to form an impression," she replied, diplomatically. "He is handsome, though his clothing is a little eccentric. He may have been nervous. I believe I should wait and form an opinion once I get to know him better."

"Those trousers were vile," exclaimed Teresa.

"You should not be looking at men's trousers," chastised their mama. Teresa had the decency to blush and look down at her hands. "But I believe you are very wise, Kathleen my dear. He may be much more charming when he is relaxed."

"I do hope so."

Surely all was not lost. He could not be all bad, could he?

Chapter 4

"Cindermaine, His Grace wants to see you." Gabriel looked up as Donnelly, a footman, stuck his head in the door of the kitchen, as he carried a delivery of fruit and vegetables in the back door for cook.

"Cindermaine, eh? It must be important if you're using my title. Well, I had better see what he wants."

Gabriel climbed up the servant's staircase and came out in the huge front foyer of his family's London mansion. One day he would be master of all this but for now, he moved silently, attempting to be as unobtrusive as possible— something that all servants strived to be. Donnelly had told him his sire was in the study. He had to avoid several delivery men bringing in large arrangements of flowers. Due to the ball this evening, the whole house had been abuzz since well before dawn. He, like all the rest of the servants, would be happy when it was over. It was just more work.

He knocked on the door of the Duke's study and stepped in when the gruff voice bade him enter. He seldom had the chance to set eyes on the man who fathered him, and he halted just inside the door, both men just drinking in the sight of their kinsman. It was just like looking into a slightly warped mirror.

"Sit." His father's instruction sounded like the way one would order a dog to behave.

"To what do I owe the pleasure, Your Grace?" asked Gabriel. He could kick himself, but he had an inability to keep his mouth shut where his sire was concerned.

While his conscience over his mother's death still pricked at him, part of him could not help feeling that the actions of a five-year-old should not be held against a twenty-five-year-old. But he could not reason with his father and it irritated Gabriel that he had never even tried to talk to the man in the past five years about the situation. He had merely accepted his place in the household and the story that had been spread among society to explain his absence during the Season.

"Cedric is ill. He has some kind of fever."

"I am sorry to hear that," replied Gabriel, assuming that was the correct thing to say. The Duke waved dismissively.

"I doubt that. Anyway, the point is, that he needs to be present at this blessed ball this evening, but he is too ill to attend. When he tries to stand up, the poor bastard practically keels over. He cannot even keep down water since he cast up his accounts all over the side of my carriage on the street yesterday. Therefore, since you are the spitting image of him, you shall have to stand in for Cedric and pretend to be him this evening."

Gabriel blinked and stared at the man who apparently was responsible for his presence in the world and wondered for a moment how it could be possible. The man was insane.

"You want me, your heir, to pretend to be your bastard son at his betrothal ball tonight, so that no one realises that the aforementioned bastard son is upstairs, casting up his accounts because he is suffering from the ague. Have I got that correct?"

"That sums it up perfectly."

"It sounds like a ridiculous comedy one might see at Drury Lane."

"What the hell do you know about Drury Lane?"

"Even the poor can go to the theatre, Pater. Do you never cast your eye down to the pit from your lofty position in your expensive box? There you shall see all sections of society mixing."

The Duke blinked then waved a dismissive hand. "Anyway, forget that. You will be dressed and ready to accept our family and friends at eight tonight. Get bathed and dressed in the blue room. You can wear Cedric's clothes."

"I do not mind wearing his coats and even those ugly waistcoats, but I am afraid my ballocks shall not be touching the inside of his inexpressibles. I doubt he would want to share them with me any more than I would want to share with him. You and I have roughly the same size feet. Presumably, you can lend me shoes and stockings. But Godfrey can take me into town for some silk breeches and a shirt. It is the least you can do for both my comfort and Cedric's."

His father leaned back in his seat and twirled his quizzing glass in his fingers, considering Gabriel's request.

"So, son, when did you grow a spine?"

"I always had one. Was having a spine and tattling on your bad behaviour, not the reason I'm sitting here in rags?"

"You are hardly in rags."

"I am not in the clothing of the heir apparent to a dukedom either."

"That was your own fault."

"The folly of a young child. A child who has more than paid the price for his loose tongue."

"You shall get your chance to go to the ball tonight, Cinderella."

"Very droll," Gabriel replied, rolling his eyes.

"Fine. Godfrey shall take you to get a shirt and silk breeches and stockings. I am sure my tailor shall have some already made. You do not look oddly shaped. Are you?"

"I have had no complaints, and all seems to be in working order. I am sure the Hartsmere line shall continue when you pop off this mortal coil and I take a young bride and produce an heir. Even if I am an old man when that happens, we both know the mamas of the *Ton* shall still queue their debutante daughters up to wed a duke."

His father harrumphed because Gabriel's words were true.

"Bugger off back to the kitchen until your brother is ready for you. I shall send down some suitable clothes for you to wear out with him. You only need a coat, waistcoat, gloves, hat and cravat to look decent." The Duke looked him up and down. "Perhaps we should get you a few outfits in case this fever Cedric has lasts a few days. You have to act like Cedric."

"I am sure I can act like a spoiled bastard son of an aristocrat. A dandy, a fop and an altogether unlikeable chap."

"Well, I cannot say I am overly fond of you, son."

"Really, Pater, I hadn't noticed. The way you shower me with gifts and affection truly overwhelms me at times."

"Shut your mouth or I shall give you a slap."

Gabriel grinned. "And mess up my pretty face before the ball? How would you explain that to Cedric's betrothed? Especially when I hit you back and you have a black eye for your troubles." The Duke paled. "Ah yes, you had forgotten, had you not? I may live under your roof and take your orders, *Your Grace*, but that is simple survival. A man must eat. But I stopped being your punching bag a long time ago. What does this girl look like and what is her name? I would not want to make an arse of myself by going to her sister or not knowing anything about her."

His father described a buxom blonde called Kathleen Roberts from America. Her father was in the ironworks and fur trades and wanted to expand into the British markets and buy an interest in English iron. A description of her willowy eighteen-year-old dark-haired sister put him at his ease. There was no way he would mistake the two sisters.

Godfrey arrived then, looking sullen and sneering in his usual foppish attire—far too much on show through his inexpressibles. Although it did make Gabriel smile. Either he was very cold, or Gabriel had been given the lion's share of the goods in the familial trouser department.

The Duke wrote a list of clothing he felt that Gabriel may need over the next few days, should Cedric remain unwell and handed it to Godfrey along with a money pouch.

"Keep an eye on him. Make sure he steals nothing and do not make any detours. I do not want him meeting people who will realise immediately he's not Cedric. They will not notice at the ball because of the candlelight and because we shall keep him away from Cedric's closest friends. But out in broad daylight, it is damned obvious he is not Cedric."

Gabriel lifted his hand and sighed. "Father, if you want me to affect a fashionable ennui to show you just how well I can imitate your eldest progeny then I can." He had added a whiny nasal quality to his voice.

"Bloody hell that is astounding," cried out Godfrey, his own fashionable ennui disappearing like melting snow from a chimney pot. "I could almost have believed Cedric was in the room just now."

The Duke had raised an eyebrow. "Yes, it is rather impressive. A little too impressive. Almost as if you do it regularly to amuse others."

Gabriel gave his father his most innocent expression which he suspected was not at all innocent. "I have no idea what you mean, Your Grace."

"I am sure you do not. Get him upstairs and into one of Cedric's coats and waistcoats then off to the tailor's before I change my mind and call this damned ball off."

"Aye, Father," said Godfrey, his voice sounding rather excitable now. Gabriel sighed and rose to his feet. It seemed his half-brother was now looking forward to the outing to the tailor. "Tally ho, Gabriel ... I mean Cedric. Let's get you suited and booted."

"I cannot wait," replied Gabriel. "Until later, *Father*."

∞   ∞   ∞

"Oh no. Not this side of hell, Cochrane. You can bugger right off," Gabriel yelled as Mr Cedric Onslow's valet walked into the blue bedchamber, a linen draped over his arm and a shaving kit, a bowl and a ewer of steaming water in his hands. "I have been bathing, shaving and dressing since I was out of leading strings. I can bloody well do all three for myself tonight too."

"My Lord," said Cochrane, his voice quiet with patient understanding as if he was talking to a petulant child, "His Grace has instructed me to act as your valet this evening and to ensure that you are turned out as a gentleman ought to be and not ... and I quote ... 'like a god-damned vagabond.'"

"I am quite capable of tying an acceptable knot in a cravat."

"My Lord, it may have escaped your notice, but your brother is, how shall I put it?"

"A fop, a dandy, an embarrassment?"

"I was going to say slightly eccentric in his attire. If you were to wear your cravat in a simple knot, no one would believe you were Mr Onslow. They would believe he had come down with something a lot more severe than a mere fever."

"Fine, but I do not need you standing over me while I wash my arse."

"Believe me, My Lord, I have no interest in your arse. While you bathe, I shall set out your clothes. We shall shave you while you are in the bath, then clip your hair a little. Mr Onslow's hair is slightly shorter than yours and we do not wish the *Ton* to be agog with news of your new hair growing tonic, now do we? But worry not, we shall make you very handsome."

Gabriel raised an eyebrow. "Are you suggesting there is something wrong with the way I look, Cochrane? Because I am not short of female company."

Cochrane chuckled as he laid out the shaving brush, soap and razor. "Oh, I know, My Lord. The maids all suffer from dreadful melancholy over the fact you seek your pleasure outside of this house."

"I am sure you and the other male servants keep them well occupied. Besides, it is not good *Ton* to tup the servants and if my sire dropped dead tomorrow, I should hate to have to fire all the maids because I had seen them all naked and vice versa."

"I hope given the fact you are about to bathe while I am in the room, the prerequisite for being fired upon your elevation to your title is not whether one has seen you naked or not."

Gabriel chuckled. "You are most definitely safe. I have no desire to tup you, Cochrane."

"Thank God."

"Amen to that."

∞   ∞   ∞

Kathleen entered Aunt Matilda's room and tip-toed over to the chaise upon which her elderly great-aunt dozed. She would just go to the old lady's jewellery case and take the necklace and earrings and not disturb her. It was for the best, or she would never have time to finish preparing for the ball. The old lady would chew her ear off.

"Kathleeeeeeen!" Aunt Matilda's cry made her jump in alarm. "Why are you creeping about my room like a highwayman?"

"I ... I do not believe highwaymen creep, Aunt Matilda. Do they not just point a pistol and demand your jewels?" Aunt Matilda thought about this for a moment, her mouth twisting first one way and then the other before she raised both eyebrows and nodded.

"I do believe you are correct, child," she chuckled. She patted her turquoise turban, fluffed the wrap that covered her legs and smiled indulgently. "Why were we talking of highwaymen? Has someone been robbed?" Her face turned ashen as she sat upright in the chaise. Kathleen hurried to her side to calm her.

"No, no. You accused me of acting like a highwayman because I was sneaking in here. I did not want to disturb you if you were sleeping. I came in because you said I should borrow your pearl necklace and earrings."

"Yes, I did, my dear." She unwound her shawl from around her shoulders and there, hanging around her neck, were about twenty necklaces, thousands of pounds worth of jewels sparkling off the candle and fire lights.

"Aunt Matilda, why are you wearing all your jewellery?"

"One can never be too careful, Kathleen. We have been here but a few weeks and we do not know half of these servants.

"But only Hattie attends you and she came over from New Hampshire with us. You know she would never steal from you."

"Of course I do," said Aunt Matilda, her brow furrowed in anger—scandalised at the mere suggestion that her faithful lady's maid would consider stealing. "But my room is seldom locked. I do not trust these English servants. They have not forgiven us for claiming our independence. Mark my words."

Kathleen chuckled. "I doubt very much if the lower classes care very much if America is independent, Aunt. If the King and the Prince Regent are reconciled to the idea and hold no grudges, then I would imagine the working classes do not care two hoots.

"Do you think?"

"Yes, I believe it is most likely."

"So do you think my jewels are safe from the servants stealing them?"

"Yes, Aunt. The gentleman who rented the house to Papa told him that all the servants are trustworthy to a fault."

"I see. Well, I shall keep them on until Hattie comes to help me to bed. You can help me off with these pearls. They shall set off your gown perfectly. That man will want to ravish you as soon as he sees you." Aunt Matilda gave Kathleen a conspiratorial wink. Kathleen hid her grimace. She was not sure she wanted Mr Onslow to ravish her. Not yet at least. Not until she got to know him and had come to terms with the idea of marriage to him. Again, she was sure he could not possibly be as bad as her first impression of him suggested.

∞   ∞   ∞

Gabriel walked into the drawing room which was crowded with members of his family and he raised an eyebrow as a hush descended. Only the family who resided in the palatial mansion on Grosvenor Square—his father, sister, and half-brother—along with Cedric's mother, the Dowager Baroness Benwick, knew he was not Cedric.

"Good evening, everyone," he drawled. "What fun. A gathering of all my richest relatives." One or two people chuckled uncomfortably, and some met his 'joke' with stony silence. A couple of elderly aunts wafted their fans more extravagantly than previously. He had hit the right note with his opening greeting. Cedric really

43

was a prize ass, and he was willing to play the prize ass up to a point, although he would take care not to offend too much where possible. He had a certain line he refused to cross. For instance, it was easier to offend gentlemen than ladies. They generally had a higher tolerance for such things due to the manner of conversations in most gentlemen's clubs and at places such as Tattersall's. He had fewer issues calling out hypocrites and cheats and those he knew treated others badly. And women he knew who were less than innocent, he would willingly tease privately for his own amusement.

One of the best things about living with servants was that one learned much more gossip about the ladies and gentlemen of the *Ton* than they thought the servants knew. While the servants made sure they never spilt the gossip about other houses to their masters or mistresses, they knew of all the goings-on in the bedchambers of almost every house in Mayfair - and what the servants knew would make the most accomplished courtesan blush.

The sound of a carriage pulling up drew Gabriel's attention to the window. This would be the Roberts family. Cedric's betrothed. What kind of young lady would she be? He doubted she would be a simpering miss—polite yet pathetic. His sire had picked this young lady for Cedric but, for all his faults, he knew the Duke to be a shrewd man. He would pick a mate who would make up for his eldest son's weaknesses, his lack of social graces perhaps, someone who could smooth ruffled feathers or keep Cedric in his place. Gabriel only had to wait a few minutes and then he would find out. He was more than a little intrigued.

The butler announced Mr and Mrs Roberts, Miss Kathleen Roberts and Miss Teresa Roberts. He stretched his neck to see past the large, round man hiding the young ladies from view. Alas, he was rotund and had not entered the room fully, so the young ladies were stuck in the doorway.

"Ah, Your Grace." He bowed low but quickly. Gabriel glimpsed a pretty and young dark-haired girl. Not the blonde he had been expecting. The sister then. Teresa. The mother curtseyed, and he spied golden curls swept up into an intricate knot.

"Please, enter. You are most welcome, Mr and Mrs Roberts." And at last, the parents of Cedric's betrothed moved out the way. His gaze alighted on the young lady whom he was to marry. He shook his head. Damn! Whom that bloody arse Cedric was to marry. What in the blazes was going on? The woman was beautiful, and she was to marry his wet fish of a half-brother. The world had gone mad. "Miss Roberts. Miss Teresa. You remember Mister Cedric Onslow, my son. Miss

Roberts, I shall allow Cedric to take you around and introduce you to everyone while I introduce your parents and sister."

"It would be my pleasure," Gabriel answered, trying for a slight superciliousness in his voice. He suspected he had failed miserably when her gaze swept up his body and she smiled, a look of relief washing over her features.

He moved over to her, offering her his sleeve. Up close she was even prettier, and her cheeks pinked as she laid her hand on his arm.

"I am pleased to see you are recovered, Mr Onslow."

"Ah yes, I believe it was something I ate which disagreed with me."

"How unfortunate for you. You did look rather peaked when you left our house. We were all quite concerned."

"Ah well, we do have very robust constitutions in our family. The Hartsmeres are descended from the Conqueror, you know. I may not be entitled to use the name, but the blood flows through my veins as much as it does in any legitimate son." God, he felt like an ass.

"I am sure it does. Would you be so kind as to introduce me to everyone?"

"Ah, yes, of course. Miss Roberts, may I introduce you to Lady Eleanor Stanbury. My Lady, Miss Kathleen Roberts, my betrothed." Gabriel's aunt looked at Gabriel and paused her quizzing glass trained on him for a few moments, her brows furrowed, then she hmphed and her expression cleared as she looked at Kathleen.

"My dear, it is a pleasure to welcome you to the family. Cedric will make a wonderful husband for you."

"Thank you very much, My Lady. And may I say what a beautiful gown you are wearing. The fabric is absolutely divine."

"Oh, this old thing. I must admit though it is my favourite. I had the fabric specially imported from India.

They made small talk for a few moments then Gabriel introduced Miss Roberts to more of his relatives. When he reached the Dowager Baroness Benwick, he stiffened.

"Lady Benwick, may I introduce Miss Roberts. Miss Roberts, my ... mother, The Dowager Baroness Benwick."

"It is a pleasure to meet you, My Lady," said Miss Roberts curtseying and showing no sign of having noticed any tension between Gabriel and Cedric's mother.

"Well, are you not just charming," said the dowager, smiling benevolently on her daughter-in-law-to-be.

"Yes, she is. Far too good for me, Mother," said Gabriel. The glare that Cedric's mother shot him could have frozen the River Thames. Gabriel had to bite the inside of his mouth to stop himself from laughing. The woman had been well aware he'd just insulted her first-born. But Miss Roberts had turned her attention to talk of soirees and musicales.

He caught his sister's gaze and Christina raised an eyebrow at him. He returned the gesture. Her gaze swept to the side and she mouthed the words *she's beautiful*. His nod was minuscule, but he knew Christina understood— so in tune were they to one another. Some people said it was because they were twins. He did not believe such poppycock. But they had a very close bond.

The fingers on his arm tightened and he understood from Miss Robert's signal that it was time to move on. He liked this about her. She was not afraid to make her needs and wishes known. He would bet that once she had lost her innocence, she would soon let a man know what she wanted in the bedroom.

He gave her a sidelong glance. Damn, why had he had to think of her in that way? She looked utterly delicious, and that mongrel Cedric would have his filthy hands all over her.

He'd heard stories about Cedric from the maids and none of them were good. It wasn't that he forced himself on them. But rather that he made such a nuisance of himself that eventually they gave in for the sake of peace. And he never considered the woman's pleasure.

"Mr Onslow. Mr Onslow." A tap on his arm brought him back from his musings about his half-brother. "I apologise, Mr Onslow, but you appeared to be wool-gathering."

"Oh, yes, I was rather. I ... perhaps I am still a little shaken by my illness."

"Ah ... Do you need to excuse yourself?"

"No, no, goodness me. Not at all. I shall be fine. Come and meet my sis ... half-sister."

Chapter 5

Kathleen walked into the ballroom on Cedric's arm. She had been quite intimidated coming to the home of a duke, but at least she was marrying his illegitimate son who was a mere Mister and so they could be paired up to enter the dining room together.

She had been relieved to arrive and see he was wearing silk evening breeches rather than inexpressibles. And he seemed lovely tonight. Less pompous. Perhaps Cedric had just been nervous yesterday. And he had been unwell. His smile seemed softer and occasionally when she caught him looking at her it was with a gleam in his eye as if he wanted to eat her. Almost the way she eyed a cream cake when she was particularly hungry. It sent a small thrill through her which settled in her belly and a little farther down. Just the thought of it made her cheeks warm.

Occasionally he had become a bit supercilious and then he seemed to forget to be so. It was almost as if it was some kind of affectation brought on by nerves, but when he was just himself, he was a thoroughly nice gentleman.

Dinner had been a charming affair. She sat between Cedric and his cousin, Mr Thomas Davenport. They had kept the discussion to polite, if rather uninteresting, topics.

Now she stood in a receiving line with her parents, the Duke, Cedric and Cedric's aunt, as the great and the good of high society congratulated her on an excellent match. One or two people gave Cedric second glances, and a few gave him a third glance, but no one said anything untoward.

"Is something wrong, Mr Onslow? A few people have been giving you odd looks."

"I cut my hair differently. That is all," he said, his tone a little sharp.

"Onslow." She looked up to see a handsome man about Onslow's age smiling at him and shaking his hand.

"Stalwood. I did not know you had been invited."

"Yes. The invitation arrived this morning. Not sure if Lady Christina had something to do with it or that servant Cinder-something. Untrustworthy fellow. You should give that one his marching orders. Put him back in his rightful place."

"I can get the footmen to throw you out, you know."

"You could, but you would never cause a scene at Miss Roberts's betrothal ball, now would you?"

"No, I would not, for Miss Roberts is much more delightful than you shall ever be Stalwood. Now, remember to behave yourself." Cedric's eyes twinkled, and his mouth twitched, as if he was trying not to smile. She suspected that these men liked each other.

Cedric formally introduced her to Lord Stalwood and His Lordship then took his leave. But as she was introduced to the Earl and Countess of Marven, she caught sight of Stalwood out of the corner of her eye approaching Lady Christina, Cedric's half-sister. Was he her suitor? She had spoken but a few sentences to the other lady, but she had found her pleasant, demure and friendly. Kathleen wondered how the various relations in this awkward family would rub along together.

"Come, all the guests are now received, apart from any latecomers. The music shall start soon. Would you like a drink before the dancing starts?" Cedric's voice was low, and he had bent to speak into her ear. His breath fluttered a curl past her ear, and it made her shiver with delight. She looked up into hazel eyes. How much lighter his eyes looked in candlelight. How odd. One would have thought they would be darker. "Is there something the matter, Miss Roberts?"

"I ... I think perhaps, given we are due to wed, that you should call me Kathleen." He smiled. It was a smug, satisfied smile.

"I would like that very much. And you should call me Gabriel."

"Gabriel?"

"Hmm? Oh." His face turned crimson, and his brows furrowed. "Uh, forget I said that. I mean Cedric. Gabriel is my middle name. I am nicknamed Gabriel, but my father hates when anyone uses it."

"Which do you prefer?"

"It is best you stick to Cedric. I would hate for you to slip up and my father to overhear."

"As you wish. Though I believe one should be called whatever one wishes, and one's father should have no say."

"Perhaps, but you shall learn that my father has an iron will and what he says goes. I suspect it is all part of being a duke."

"And is your half-brother like that? The one who will inherit the title?"

"Gabriel? Oh no."

"Gabriel?"

"Yes, that is his name." He looked at her and then closed his eyes as he seemed to understand her confusion. "Gabriel is also my father's first name. My mother wanted me called after him but because I'm a ba ... I am illegitimate. He was not willing to call me after himself. My half-brother's mother was more successful in that endeavour with his heir."

"I see. So that may be why your father dislikes you being called Gabriel."

"Yes, perhaps."

"Well, I believe you are correct that calling you Cedric is for the best at present, but perhaps we can revisit that once we are better acquainted. I want you to be happy and comfortable with me."

He looked down at her, a quizzical look in his gaze, then his frustration appeared to wane and his gaze softened as he smiled at her. "I believe I was correct when I spoke to the Dowager earlier. You are far too good for Cedric Onslow, my dear. Have a glass of champagne." He stopped a passing footman and picked two glasses of champagne from the silver tray the man carried. He offered one to her and she accepted it with a little nod. The man seemed to speak in riddles, but he also sent warmth through her. Was this the desire she had read about in novels?

∞   ∞   ∞

Gabriel could not believe his slip. What an idiot he had been to give her his own first name. Cedric might have some explaining to do at the altar when Kathleen found out his real middle name was Peregrine. That was not Gabriel's problem, however. He had not asked to be part of this charade. As a servant, he merely did as he was told.

But he felt bad for deceiving Kathleen. He liked the chit, as much as he had seen of her. She had made polite chit-chat through dinner, but she seemed to have picked up that he did not want to give much of himself away and had respected that. Women tended to be nosey, curious creature by nature, and he was sure she was dying to find out more about her husband-to-be. But she was patiently biding her time.

Kathleen was also beautiful. Something which made him uncomfortable as he led her onto the dance floor and slipped his hand around her slender waist. As he took her gloved hand in his, her breath hitched, and her blue gaze met his. Despite two layers of silk between their palms, he was aware of the heat between them.

He forced himself to maintain the appropriate distance between their bodies. It had been a long time since he had wanted a woman so much. Was it because she was the forbidden fruit—another thing denied to him by his cruel father? Was it because he felt that as the legitimate heir, she should be his?

Of course, having been raised both above and below stairs, he did not have the same sense of entitlement that many ducal heirs possessed, and he did not view women as property.

He smiled at her as he led her off into the waltz, twirling her down the line of dancers. She was graceful and elegant as all young ladies were taught to be, but not all achieved.

"You dance divinely, Kathleen."

"As do you, Cedric."

"You flatter me. Do they waltz much in New Hampshire?"

"Not much. In Boston, yes. Since I grew up, I spend more time there. That is where most of society is. Papa goes to New Hampshire because that is where his business interests are—his iron works."

"And London is to your taste?"

"Oh yes. It is much warmer than Massachusetts and New Hampshire. The snow will be heavy there now."

"So you would have to wrap up warm."

"Oh yes. Carriage rides are out of the question. We use sleighs and ponies and we walk many places too. That is why it is good to be in town. It is lonely in the country at this time of year."

"I would imagine it is." He would not mind being snowed in with the delectable Miss Roberts though. In fact, as her tongue darted out to lick the bow of her lips, he had to tamp down his reaction to her.

"Do you mind that your father found you a wife?" she asked without preamble. "I mean ..." Her cheeks flushed a delightful shade of pink and she bit her lip for a moment as he supposed she must be reconsidering the propriety of her words.

"Go on," he urged.

"Well, is it common among the *Ton* to arrange marriages in such a manner? For us to be at our betrothal ball when we have only met once?"

Now she bit her lip in earnest and looked over his shoulder, unable to meet his gaze.

"Kathleen, I do not mind you asking. And normally we would have at least got to know each other. Yes, many marriages are arranged, but usually the families encourage the couple to court and see if they suit. That said, most young ladies are schooled to be rather unremarkable so they would suit most men, I suppose."

"Rather unremarkable?"

He frowned, not knowing how to explain it in such a way that would not sound so unkind. "Society expects young ladies to behave in such a manner that they are benign and inoffensive. Their dresses are demure, they all play the pianoforte or the harp or sing. They all do embroidery. They visit the subscription library and ride during the fashionable hour. But none must stand out. Those who stand out either find love matches or end up as spinsters, bluestockings or scandalous young misses. But mostly, one young lady is much like all the others. They are all rather like buckskin breeches. Give or take a couple of inches at the waist, they all fit a gentleman perfectly and look almost the same."

"Oh Mr Onslow, that is a terrible thing to say." When he looked into her eyes, he could see she was rather scandalised.

"Yes, it is rather. It is true, nonetheless. The waltz is finishing, and I must take you back to your Mama. I may not claim another dance with you until the supper dance. I shall write my name on your dance card, assuming that is acceptable. But, watch the young ladies, especially the ones in white and pastel shades. You will see exactly what I mean."

He led her over to the group of older ladies where Kathleen's mother stood along with her young sister. The girl was not officially out yet and could not waltz, but she could do a country dance. He wrote his name on Kathleen's dance card for the supper dance, then on Teresa's for a country dance just prior to the supper dance and a cotillion later in the evening. His duties done, he bowed elegantly to Mrs Roberts and her companions and set off in search of someone whom he might converse with and with whom he would not get into trouble.

∞   ∞   ∞

"She thinks I'm a god-damned monster." Gabriel moaned to his sister and his former friend.

"Really," hissed Christina, smiling beatifically at one of the *grande dames* who was scowling as she strolled by with one of her compatriots. "Polite society," she emphasised with a gesture of her head to the now whispering ladies.

Gabriel scowled and shook his own head. "They think I'm Cedric. Honestly Chrissie, surely that is the least offensive thing he says."

Christina rolled her eyes. "He does not take the Lord's name in vain. He is just ..." she waved her hand as if unsure how to express herself.

"Ill-mannered, as subtle as a coach and four, as demure as Prinny?"

"Something like that," she conceded. "But he does not curse."

"He does now."

"Fine, so why does she think you are a monster?"

He recounted the conversation on the dance floor.

"Really, Gabe, how did we share the same space during our mother's confinement without me throttling you?"

"Christ, you two do not understand polite ballroom conversation, do you?" said Stalwood.

"Says the man taking our saviour's name in vain," said Gabriel, a smile tugging at his lips.

"Touché."

"I shall smooth things over with Miss Roberts. You two try to stay away from Cedric's vile friends. I see Mr Lawrence Appleby heading this way. He shall try to encourage you to go to a gaming hell and a brothel after the ball if you are not careful," said Christina.

"What do you know of broth ... oh never mind." Gabriel did not have time to ask about his sister's knowledge of the more nefarious activities of their elder half-brother and the seedier side of London's nightlife. Lawrence Appleby was indeed bearing down on them, his inexpressibles giving the ladies in the ballroom quite a view. It seemed Lawrence was a little aroused. And now Gabriel had that vision in his head.

"I believe Lady Stewart is calling us over," he said to Stalwood, steering his friend in the opposite direction.

"She is?"

"She is," he said, his voice a warning growl.

∞   ∞   ∞

Kathleen looked around and saw Lady Christina heading her way. She smiled at the woman and closed her fan then curtseyed to her. Lady Christina curtseyed back.

"Would you like to take a turn about the ballroom with me, Miss Roberts?"

"Oh, thank you. I would. No one has solicited my hand for this dance."

They moved away from her sister and mama and once they were out of earshot Christina asked, "Are you enjoying the ball?"

"I am. Very much so."

"And how do you find my half-brother?" Christina looked over towards a little nook and Kathleen's gaze followed and sure enough, there was Cedric bowing over the hand of an elderly matron. The woman looked a little confused. Then she scowled.

"Ah, yes, he is nice."

"I believe he is concerned that he has offended you."

"Oh?" She could not say any more. His comments about all young ladies being like men's breeches was a little insulting.

"He explained his comment about the breeches." Christina rolled her eyes. "Honestly. I despair of Gabriel."

"You call him Gabriel."

"Uh ... I ..."

"He told me your father does not approve. He told me that his mother wanted to call him Gabriel but your father wanted to reserve that name for his legitimate heir, so it is his middle name and Cedric became his first name. And your other brother's name is Gabriel."

"Yes, he is."

"He lives in the country does he not? I heard he is in poor health. Is that not so?"

"Something like that."

Christina was watching Cedric again.

"We were talking about Cedric comparing young ladies to breeches," Kathleen prompted, deciding it was time to get the conversation back to the subject that Christina had come to discuss.

"Yes. Well, all he meant was that in society, we are all taught the same things. We all learn the same manners and polite conversation is terribly uninteresting. I am not saying that no one has a personality. We do. But we can be moulded to fit almost any gentleman if necessary. That, sadly, is why so many young ladies end up married to men thirty years their senior."

"I see."

"He did not mean to be uncouth. He was just trying to explain the way of the *Ton* albeit in a rather brutish manner."

"I understand."

"He worries he has offended you."

"He has not."

"Good, because he is here to claim you for the supper dance."

∞   ∞   ∞

"How was your waltz?" Stalwood asked Gabriel, referring to the supper dance. They stood at the buffet choosing food and adding it to plates for the ladies and themselves while Kathleen and Christina were sitting at a table together talking animatedly. Gabriel cast a glance at his former dance partner.

"Mostly it went well. I could relax and speak with her and flirt a little this time. Until she suggested we go out riding the day after tomorrow. In the park."

"Riding?"

"Yes. On horses."

Stalwood barked out a laugh. "Yes Cindermaine, I am au fait with the general principle of riding."

"Perhaps, but when one has barely had two farthings to rub together for most of his adult life, where do you suppose one gets hold of decent horseflesh?"

Stalwood halted, a slice of beef halfway between the serving salver and the plate he was holding. "Oh, I see what you mean." Gabriel nudged him back to his task. "What about the duke? Does he not have a horse you could borrow?"

"He never rides when in town. Only in the country. He conveys his mistress about in a closed carriage—for the sake of propriety—if you can believe it. He acknowledges her bastard sons, everyone knows about them, but he uses a closed carriage for reasons that no one else can fathom." He placed some sweet meats on a plate.

"All the horses in his stable are carriage horses. Carriage horses are dreadful for riding, especially in a park full of people. They are used to harnesses, not someone on their back in a saddle. You are an excellent horseman. I need not tell you how different it would be. The last thing I want is to be thrown off a horse in front of Miss Roberts and land on my arse in the middle of the Serpentine. She already thinks I'm a dolt."

"I can understand. You can borrow Thunder."

"Thunder! You still have that stallion?"

"Yes."

"Why?" Gabriel asked, astounded

"He likes the ladies." Stalwood defended.

"So do I, but no one would put up with the kind of behaviour from me that your stallion exhibits."

"Actually, they would because you are a duke's son."

Gabriel considered that.

"Well possibly, but half the young ladies of the *Ton* would have broken limbs and would be increasing to boot."

"You have missed your opportunity, old chap."

"Mayhap, but back to the horse. I will not ride that brute. It is a damned menace. If you had any sense, you would chop its ballocks off and calm it down."

"Here now, that is a bit harsh on the poor chap. What did he ever do to you?"

"I could not sit down for a month after he threw me five years ago. I am sure he broke something in my backside."

"Ah, best not then. The chances of you ending up in the Serpentine are definitely increased if you take Thunder."

"Definitely. Listen, did I see you talking to Viscount Beattie earlier."

"Ah, yes. Beattie is a good fellow. I... think we should talk about Beattie another time. Come, we had better get back to the ladies. They appear to be wilting from lack of nourishment."

They hurried over to the ladies who looked up, almost surprised to see their arrival.

"Kathleen and I are arranging a visit to the modiste soon. We are also discussing which *at homes* we should attend, to which balls we should drag you and to what other entertainments for the rest of the Christmas season we can subject you," stated Christina airily.

"You forget, sister, that I am indisposed for the next week."

"No you are not. I promised Kathleen I would take her to Gunther's for an ice."

"An ice, at this time of year?" asked Stalwood, taking the words right out of Gabriel's mouth. "It's freezing, in case you hadn't noticed. If you order an ice, they'll cart you off to Bedlam."

"Christina, I have that thing I must do."

"Father will understand now you are betrothed. Do not worry. I have the situation in hand."

Christina gave him one of her soothing looks and Gabriel was torn. He wanted to throttle his twin, but he wanted to trust her too. He glanced at Kathleen who had no idea what a tangled web was being spun around her and she sliced into her roast beef, looked up and bestowed a sunny smile upon him. Those rosy lips were so innocent, so wet, so kissable. Could he find a secluded area to take her to? Should he? He knew this house like the back of his hand. Finding the perfect spot would not be an issue. The morality of doing it, however, was another matter.

When supper was over and Christina had finished her incessant chattering about bonnets and frills and which modiste was the best, Stalwood held him back from the ladies as they re-entered the ballroom.

"Meet me at Tattersall's at midday tomorrow, old chap. We'll get you a gelding. Wouldn't want that pretty little arse of yours getting all wet and your other cheeks turning all red in front of the delectable Miss Roberts. Besides, Thunder needs someone to race."

"Oh no. You are not buying me a horse."

"Damned right I'm not. The duke will buy you a horse. I'm off to speak to him. I see your sister's hand has been claimed. Keep an eye on her. I would hate any harm to come to her from some overly eager young buck. Your sister needs a proper gentleman who knows how to treat her properly."

"What, like you?" Gabriel chuckled. But the laugh died in his throat as he saw the way Stalwood's gaze narrowed on the gentleman kissing Christina's hand. "You want to court my sister, Stalwood." It wasn't a question.

"She makes me smile," he said simply.

Gabriel nodded. Somehow such a simple reason made sense. "Miss Roberts, would you like to take a turn about the ballroom?" he asked, before his own young lady was accosted for a dance. The colour that rose in her cheeks was delightful and she fumbled with her fan. Was she really attracted to him? Damn! Would she be more or less attracted to him if she knew he was an earl? Titles always made women swoon. What a damn shame he could not use his title to impress her.

"Thank you, Mr Onslow." She placed her gloved hand on his sleeve, and he stepped towards the edge of the room.

"Your sister is lovely. Do you mind her inviting me out to visit the modiste with her?"

"Why should I mind?"

"Well, I had been led to believe that the two sides of the family did not get on."

"That has been the case in the past, but the family is changing. Perhaps one day I may even get on with my half-brother."

"He is the duke's heir. Are you and he alike?"

"Those who know my half-brother and me say that physically we are like two peas in a pod."

"Are you alike in temperament?"

Gabriel hated where this conversation was heading. Cedric was an arse. He was sure he had some less than desirable qualities, but he was also certain that as a man he beat his half-brother hands down. But what could he say?

"We have had very different upbringings. It shaped us into different types of gentlemen."

Kathleen frowned. "I see." It was clear that she really did not see.

It was better just to leave the conversation where it was though and not press things any further. His sire had created this ridiculous mess, and the Duke had to accept that he would make mistakes.

They nodded at acquaintances but did not stop to speak to anyone. Gabriel tried his best to appear besotted with his bride—something that was not too difficult to achieve. She was beautiful. He could not engage in conversation with any of Cedric's friends. They would know immediately that he was not Cedric and jig would be up.

The door to the conservatory was close. He had to get out of this crowd. Gabriel drew Kathleen to the edge of the ballroom and tried the handle of the door. It opened easily.

He touched his gloved finger to his lips and gave Kathleen a conspiratorial raise of his eyebrows. Her own lips twitched, and she glanced around as if expecting someone to catch them in the act of sneaking away. Gabriel stepped into the cool room, drawing his companion with him, before catching the inside handle and closing the door with a *snick.*

There were candles burning in the wall sconces and floating candles in the ornamental fountain in the middle of the conservatory. His father had good taste. For all his faults, the man had style. How the family's sense of style had so badly skipped the duke's eldest and youngest sons was a mystery to Gabriel. Kathleen's bright eyes and parted lips were a testament to just how beautiful the plethora of flowers was. While the number of flowers was diminished because it was December there were still many flowers for the season. Reds, yellows and oranges with a few purples and blues. Foliage hung everywhere, and the scent of pollen hit Gabriel's nostrils.

"It is beautiful. Thank you for bringing me in here."

"Thank you for coming with me." Gabriel moved in front of her, blocking her view of the conservatory. She raised her face, her rose petal lips stretching into a wary smile. Oh, she suspected what was coming next but was she excited, nervous, or was she horrified?

"Kathleen, would it be very inappropriate for me to try to kiss you?"

"Try? Have you never kissed a young lady before?"

He chuckled. "Try may have been the wrong word. I assure you, I am quite practised in the art."

"Then I apologise that I am quite untutored, Cedric."

"Call me Gabriel, please. When we are alone."

He did not care if she made a mistake. He would gladly take a beating from his sire in order to hear her say his name at this moment. He just could not bear her to call him the same name as his ass of a brother when he was about to taste those cherry red lips.

"I shall—Gabriel."

"Much better," he whispered, against her lips.

His thumb stroked her jaw, his fingers helping to angle her head as his lips caressed hers. Warmth flooded his belly, but he held himself back. Kathleen moved her lips over his experimentally and Gabriel had to quash a groan of need. For a first kiss, Kathleen needed a gentle introduction to the feelings he could draw from her, not a mauling as his brother would have given her. And then he forced the thoughts of his half-brother out of his mind and surrendered to the softness of her lips.

Kathleen sighed as she parted her lips and Gabriel allowed his hand to drift around her neck so that he did not disturb her coiffure and have people gossiping about her. He pressed his tongue inside her mouth and eased himself a step closer, sliding his free hand around her waist.

Devil take it. She tasted delicious. And she learned quickly.

Her hands grazed over his waistcoat and up his chest before slipping around his neck as he swept his tongue around her mouth. She copied his movements naturally. He forced his hand to remain on her waist. The man in him wanted to move it down and urge her bottom closer until she rubbed against his growing hardness. But the gentleman in him knew this was her first kiss and his needs and desires were secondary.

Kathleen moaned and pushed herself onto tiptoes. Tilting her head and adjusting the position, deepening the kiss still further. God's teeth. He had not been this affected by a mere kiss since ... well, he never had been this affected by a kiss.

He withdrew until their lips barely touched and then he pulled away completely.

Her lips pursed, Kathleen tried to follow him. It was almost comical. Then she seemed to realise the kiss was over and she opened her eyes, looking somewhat dazed and a little disappointed. He touched his forehead to hers. His own disappointment as keen as hers. He was just better at faking it. He needed a moment to recover his wits, and it had to be time not gazing into those crystal-clear blue eyes.

"Was your first kiss enjoyable, Kathleen?"

"It was … wonderful, Ced—Gabriel."

"I too thought it was wonderful. I wish we had time to prolong this assignation, but we have to get back."

"May I just apologise for the sound I made? I do not know what came over me. The feelings …"

He lifted his head and shook it. She stopped speaking and gave him a quizzical look.

"Never apologise for any sounds you make that are borne of pleasure. A sound like that gives a man heart that the lady is enjoying a gentleman's kisses."

Her lips moved into a delightful little 'o' shape, and he was tempted to pull her into another kiss. But he was not convinced that a second time he could be in such control. He was already growing hard with want and would have to think of Cedric in his inexpressibles to ensure that he got rid of the slight bulge in his silk breeches before going back into the ballroom.

Yes, the thought of Cedric's inexpressibles was definitely working already.

"Thank you for your kindness."

"There was no kindness involved. The pleasure was all mine. Let us take a quick turn around the flower beds so our colour can return to normal. You look a little flushed. Then I shall return you to your mama."

"Thank you. You are obviously quite practised at secret assignations with young ladies."

He gave her a sidelong glance. Was that jealousy he heard in her voice?

"No, not really."

"Oh, come now, Mr Onslow. You are a very handsome gentleman. The ladies must throw themselves at you."

"But you forget. I am a ba ... I am illegitimate."

"But the recognised son of a duke."

"Mayhap but most mamas want at least a baron for their daughters. I shall never have a title unless I save the life of the Prince Regent himself."

"That does seem a little unfair."

"Ah, the vagaries of the hereditary peerage were never said to be fair, Miss Roberts."

And with that, he opened the door to the hothouse and swept her back out into the ballroom.

Chapter 6

"How the devil did you manage it?" Gabriel asked, feeling the pouch of coins in his pocket once again as they walked towards Hyde Park and Tattersall's auction.

"I just explained to your father how little he wanted society to know about his heir being kept as a servant while he treats his bastard sons better than the Prince Regent, and allows them to gad about town, often lording it over ... well ... actual lords. Your brothers are not well liked from what I hear."

"Godfrey seems ..." Gabriel waved his free hand. "Oh, I don't know ... pliable ... as if someone could reform the poor bugger. He laughed at my Cedric impersonation. And when it was just him and me in the carriage, he dropped his fashionable ennui and became almost human. It is as if no one ever taught him how not to act like an ass."

"It is likely that no one did. He only had your father and Cedric to look up to and his mother is …"

"She is evil."

"Is she? That is a pretty strong word, Gabe."

"She was evil to Christina. I think my punishment was her idea too. She never forgave us for being born even though we had no choice. My mother and father's marriage was arranged as far as I can tell, though my father was in love with the daughter of a mere knight, and that was not good enough for his father. No matter that she was pretty and has a big bosom and loved my father back. Or that he had already ruined her."

"You noticed your step-mother has a big bosom?" asked Myles.

"She's not my step-mother. She never married my father. And of course I noticed. She does not hide it under a shawl. The woman does not know how to be demure. Do not say you did not notice."

"Well, of course, but one never likes to mention it."

"They are not something one can miss. A bit like her sons'… well, you know … in their inexpressibles."

"It is the ladies I feel sorry for. They must find it so difficult to know where to look."

"Well not down there, I would wager."

"Ah, here we are, now, let's see if we can get you a decent gelding."

"I shall not be taking advice from you on horseflesh. Not after the state of my arse after that brute of yours threw me."

They entered Tattersall's and Gabriel breathed in the smell of horse manure and hay. He had not been here since his university days. It felt wonderful to have some freedom again.

∞　∞　∞

"Now we are alone, you can tell me honestly what you think of Gab ... I mean Cedric," Christina said to Kathleen as the carriage made its way to Bond Street and Lady Christina's favourite modiste.

"Oh, umm ..."

"Ha, there is no need to be coy. He is only my half-brother, and I would never say a word to him."

"I like him exceedingly well. I must admit I was not sure upon first meeting him the other day when he came to our house to arrange the betrothal ball, but the poor man was not well. But at the ball, he was ... charming."

"Charming? Indeed. I did notice you disappeared into the hothouse for a while with him."

Heat crawled up Kathleen's neck. "Oh?"

"I did. Only because I had feigned a turned ankle during my dance so that I could get away from my horrible dance partner to be with Myles and we wanted to sneak off but you and Gab … Cedric were already in there."

"Myles?"

"Lord Stalwood."

"Oh. I … oh. You and Lord Stalwood are on given name terms. You are planning to wed?"

"Well, neither of us has mentioned it but we do like each other exceedingly well and we deal nicely together. We are currently working on a … a … how do I put it … a project together."

"A project?"

"Yes. I believe I have said enough on the matter, however. It is supposed to be a secret. One day I shall tell you and you shall be as delighted as I am."

How intriguing. Lady Christina was like a heroine in a novel, full of secrets and passions. Kathleen would not be surprised if she burned with desire for Lord Stalwood, though Kathleen was not quite sure what burning with desire felt like. She did wonder though if she had been given a taste of it with Cedric last night.

"Ah, here we are. Madame Leclerc. She has the most delightful fabrics that will show off your décolletage perfectly. My poor brother will not know where to place his gaze. What fun. I do love tormenting the poor soul."

She chuckled as the footman handed her down from the carriage then she waited as he helped Kathleen to disembark too.

Lady Christina was correct. Madame Leclerc had the most beautiful fabrics, many imported from the East. Christina and she looked through the fashion plates and Christina, who insisted that Kathleen drop the honorific, urged her to purchase a few new gowns for the Christmas season. They also as good as chose her wedding gown, but Kathleen explained to Christina that she would have to bring her mother back for the final decision.

"I could never purchase my wedding gown without my mother seeing what I was going to wear. She has been looking forward to this day for so long."

"Oh, is that an American idea? We choose a nice gown for our wedding day, but it is not so special we would insist our mama helped in the final decision."

Kathleen laughed. "I do not think so. I think it is just me."

"Well, I think it is lovely and Gab … Cedric will not be able to take his gaze from you."

A warmth grew in Kathleen's belly along with a little knot of worry. The kiss had made her light-headed and given her butterflies in her stomach, but she still remembered him standing in front of her with those inexpressibles on and his anatomy fully visible underneath. It had not been threatening in the least. It just did not inspire the kind of thoughts his kisses had.

"Kathleen, you seem unwell. We have finished anyway. Come, let us step outside for some air. It is rather warm and stuffy in here."

Christina led Kathleen by the elbow out of the modiste's shop and onto Bond Street. It was rather busy, and Kathleen sucked in her breath as the cool air hit her lungs.

"Oh, it is rather fresh today."

"Yes, it is a little chilly. Never fear we have lots of shops to visit."

Christina led Kathleen down the busy shopping street visiting several shops and purchasing all manner of things. By the time Christina declared them finished, the poor footman was laden under boxes of bonnets and gloves and jewellery.

"Shall we walk to Gunther's for tea, or shall we walk back to the carriage? It is a little cold. I would not want you catching a chill before your wedding," said Christina, looking with concern at Kathleen.

"Cold? This is like summer compared to New Hampshire in winter. I do not mind walking, but if you would prefer the carriage, I would understand."

"Nonsense. Never let it be said the British were afraid of a little cold. Tomkins, go back to the carriage and tell the driver to meet us at Gunther's." The footman nodded, looked around, but hesitated and did not seem keen to leave the ladies alone. "Honestly Tomkins, no one will accost us in Mayfair."

"Chrissie." They both turned, and Kathleen caught her breath as she looked up into dark eyes. She dared not look down for fear that the handsome man who enthralled her so was wearing those dreadful inexpressibles. "Miss Roberts."

Christina batted her half-brother with her parasol. "Would you not yell Chrissie at me in the street? It is so uncouth." She then turned to the footman. "See? A couple of rogues with whom we are well acquainted have already accosted us. We are quite safe. Lord Stalwood, how delightful to see you again. Would you accompany us to Gunther's?"

"It would be our pleasure," said Lord Stalwood, bowing to Lady Christina. He offered her his sleeve and Christina took it with alacrity. Cedric offered his sleeve to Kathleen, and she accepted graciously though with less enthusiasm lest he think her fast.

As they set off down the street, Cedric spoke. "Did you enjoy last night?"

"Oh, exceedingly well. The ballroom was beautiful, and the dancing was such fun."

"Ah yes, the ball. That was entertaining too." She looked up to his face and could see his mouth twitching as if he was trying not to chuckle. Was he thinking of their interlude in the hothouse?

"Mr Onslow, are you having a private reminiscence?"

"You are welcome to join me, Miss Roberts."

Despite the cold, Kathleen felt a warmth spread up from her belly. "Mr Onslow, stop being so scandalous in public."

"Once we are wed, I shall be much more scandalous in private, my love."

His voice was so quiet she knew only she could hear him, but it still sent a thrill of excitement through her.

"Please, Mr Onslow. That is quite improper for public discussion."

"I know. That is why only you can hear me, Miss Roberts. Fear not, I would never subject you to public scandal."

"Like your father has done to your mother?" As soon as she had said the words, Kathleen wished she could take them back. Cedric's jaw tightened, and he looked ahead as if considering a polite way to reply. She was just about to apologise for her *faux pas* when he spoke.

"Lady Benwick and the Duke of Hartsmere and their personal lives are none of my concern. The *Ton* excuse the behaviour of dukes because they are a mere step down from princes and the *Ton* are hypocrites. You, as an American and a commoner, have no such cushion from their wrath. But as charming and clever as you are, I do not doubt you will have all the *grande dames* wrapped around your finger in no time and the scandal of the birth of the Duke of Hartsmere's eldest child will be nought more than a footnote in Debrett's."

Kathleen thought it a little odd that Cedric sometimes referred to himself in the third person. It was always when he was discussing his family situation. She wondered if he was uncomfortable discussing it. She decided not to mention it again. It did not do to make one's betrothed feel uncomfortable.

They soon arrived at Gunther's. The place was quiet, due to it being the Christmas Season. Few people travelled to town for the festivities since the roads were usually impassable by carriage.

The gentlemen led them to seats and a waiter took their order. Just as the conversation was turning to topics other than the weather, a couple of dandies arrived at their table.

"Cedric, old chap. Missed you last night. It was a real hoot. We were all in our cups. Neville here almost mistook this young lad for a tart."

"Henry, there are ladies present. Do you mind?" said Mr Onslow in a low voice.

The man called Neville took out his quizzing glass and appeared to inspect Kathleen and Christina through it. His nose crinkled, and his voice turned more nasal than it had already been. "Your affianced bride and your half-sister? Really Cede, she shall have to get used to your ways. You shall not be faithful, for God's sake. That is so ... lower class."

Cedric seemed to bat his friends away like flies. "I don't know Hen. I find I am tiring of my old ways. Do you not find the life of an indolent wastrel to be somewhat intolerable? I am bored. And Miss Roberts is scintillating company."

Kathleen felt uncomfortable as Cedric's friends leered at her.

"I say you must have had a bump on the head, old chap," put in Neville.

"Mayhap. Or mayhap marriage shall agree with me," said Cedric

"I am never letting my Mama pick out a bride for me. That is it." Neville shuddered.

The gentlemen said their goodbyes just as the ices arrived.

"Well, that is a positive outcome at least," piped up Christina.

"What is that, my dear?" asked Lord Stalwood. Kathleen watched in fascination as Lord Stalwood's gaze remained transfixed on Christina's lips as she licked the ice from her spoon. Christina laid her spoon down and beamed at him.

"No poor chit will be forced to marry that vile brute."

"You sound like you have had a run in with him, Chrissie."

Christina shrugged. "Nothing I did not get myself out of."

"Chrissie, what happened?" growled Cedric.

"What did he do?" barked Lord Stalwood, his hands balling into fists.

"He asked to kiss me on the terrace of someone's ballroom and when I refused, he decided he would kiss me anyway. So I hit him with my knee between his legs."

Everyone around the table looked at Christina wide-eyed.

"You mean you kneed him where a young lady should not even know to knee a gentleman?"

Cedric asked, his lips pursed as if he was struggling not to laugh.

"I knew to knee him there because I did it to you a time or two when we were children, *Cedric*."

Cedric grimaced. "Ah yes. You always were a violent little thing."

"Only to you, my darling."

"Oh, you grew up together," Kathleen asked. She had thought they had grown up apart.

Cedric and Christina looked at one another and Lord Stalwood cleared his throat.

"Cedric and his brother came to live with us when Gabriel and I were about three. It was before our mother died. That is when our father recognised Cedric and Godfrey as his sons."

Cedric gave a slight nod of his head to Christina, and she appeared to relax. Kathleen felt that once again she had intruded upon something she should have stayed out of.

"I apologise. I should not have asked. Please if I ask anything you feel is intrusive or inappropriate, do feel free to say so."

Cedric lifted her hand in his and raised it to his lips. "My dear, sweet Kathleen, we will be wed soon and there should be no secrets between us." Once again he caught his sister's gaze and a significant look passed between them. Kathleen was feeling terribly uncomfortable, and she wasn't sure it was all to do with Cedric making her heart flutter—though he was.

"Christina, I wonder if I may trouble you to go home now. I feel a little light-headed. I fear the British weather is still a little unusual as I am used to extreme cold or extreme heat. This damp, cool weather does not yet agree with me."

"Yes, of course. I do hope you are not coming down with whatever Cedric had."

"Cedric said it was something he ate."

"Likely so, but one never knows."

"True."

Chapter 7

"She knows," Gabriel ground out as he sat atop his horse awaiting Miss Roberts and her groom.

"How can she know? For goodness' sake, Gabriel. No one could imagine that such a ridiculous set of circumstances could be playing out in the middle of Mayfair in the Christmas Season. It sounds more like a Drury Lane production," Christina reasoned.

"That is exactly what I told the Duke."

"You mean Father?"

"I mean the Duke. He is not and never has been a father to me, Chrissie. I have no fond memories to tell of, just scars where the blaggard whipped me and left marks."

Chrissie's gloved hand flew to her mouth and Gabriel regretted his words immediately. He'd never told her about the beatings but he'd assumed she knew because he'd abused Chrissie when she was young too.

"Does he still beat you?"

"No. Not since I punched back. I'm sorry, Christina, I should not have told you that."

"Of course you should have told me. You should have told me when it was happening. Devil take it, Gabe. The man's a monster."

"Christina, settle down. You are frightening the horses and the ladies in their carriages." Gabriel stifled a laugh as Stalwood rode up beside his sister and laid a comforting hand on hers encouraging her to loosen her grip on her reins.

Gabriel frowned then. His friend was far too comfortable with his sister. Christina was an innocent. At least he damned well hoped she was.

"Cindermaine?" Gabriel looked up at Stalwood when his friend used his title.

"Best not to call me that. Might confuse things."

"You're the Earl of Cindermaine, Gabriel, and I shall not call you anything different when we're alone. You have always been Cindermaine to me. Anyway, why do you glower at us as if you want to kill me?"

"You are touching my sister."

Christina snorted. "You have never been protective of me before. I have been to balls, soirees, at homes, garden parties. Even Vauxhall Gardens and you have never cared two hoots whether gentlemen touched me."

"Who touched you and I shall run them through with a damned sword?"

Christina rolled her eyes.

"I have been kissed."

"Oh, you have, Lady Christina. I am disappointed to know I shall not be your first."

Christina beamed at Myles. "But perhaps you shall be my last and the one I like the most."

"You will not be kissing my sister," Gabriel growled.

Christina raised an imperious eyebrow at him as his horse danced to the side. Whether it was because he had gripped the reins tighter or because he'd raised his voice, Gabriel could not be sure but, with a nudge of his knee, he brought the beast back under control.

"You do not have a say, Lord Cindermaine. You are younger than I am."

"By eight minutes, you obnoxious little chit."

She turned to Stalwood and grinned. "I do believe even if I did not want you to kiss me, Lord Stalwood, I would allow it, just to watch my poor brother turn that dreadful colour. Poor lamb."

The sound of slow hoofbeats which suggested a lady rider was approaching saved Gabriel from further teasing by his sister. He turned his mount and was delighted to see a vision in forest green. A jaunty little hat with a large feather sat on her golden hair and her cheeks were pink with the cold.

An ache settled in Gabriel's chest. How was he going to let this darling creature go when the real Cedric was well enough? And how could he let that bastard put his grubby hands on her?

Her gaze raked up his body, settling first on his thighs which hugged his new black gelding, keeping the creature steady. Riding a horse again after so long had come so naturally. Gabriel had been shocked about how comfortable he was to be back in the saddle. They had picked a well-tempered beast, unlike Stalwood's creature, who stamped with impatience and snorted. Why anyone would purchase a stallion for anything but breeding was beyond Gabriel. Thunder was nought but a menace. The beast had obviously taken a shine to Christina's mare, which Gabriel was no happier about than the shine that Thunder's owner had taken to Gabriel's sister.

Gabriel noticed a look of relief settling on Miss Robert's face as she admired his buff riding breeches. Then he remembered the inexpressibles favoured by his half-brother. It seemed the young woman preferred her gentlemen to not have all his attributes, such as they were in Cedric's case, out on display for the entire *Ton* to see. He wondered if there was a way to convince Cedric to give up wearing the vile garments for Kathleen's sake.

"Good afternoon, gentlemen. Lady Christina."

"Good afternoon, Miss Roberts. It is lovely to see you again. Shall we go down to the Serpentine and see if Lord Stalwood's horse will do us the honour of tossing him in for our amusement?"

She gave Myles a cheeky grin, and he pursed his lips in mock ennui.

They all turned their mounts in the direction of the Serpentine but had barely moved a few steps when they heard men's voices call out Cedric's name. Gabriel closed his eyes and continued to ride on, but Kathleen stopped.

"Mr Onslow, those gentlemen are calling you."

"Are they? Oh, so they are. I must have been wool-gathering." Gabriel gave Stalwood a knowing look and pulled his hat further down over his eyes. He turned and sneered at the younger men who rode up, looking excited to see Cedric.

"Onslow, we thought you refused to ride."

Damn, he had not thought of the problem of Cedric's fear of horses. A big Clydesdale had kicked his half-brother in the ballocks when he was around sixteen on Lord Benwick's estate and Cedric had refused to ride since. It was ridiculous really. Everyone had been at the wrong end of an argument with an angry horse at some time or other.

Gabriel waved his hand dismissively and made sure to speak through his nose, and to sound a little bored. "It is not that I cannot ride, but rather that I choose not to ride. But Miss Roberts was keen and what Miss Roberts wants, Miss Roberts gets."

"Devil take it, Onslow, but your leg-shackle seems like a dreadfully snug fit already. Are you certain this is a good idea?" Gabriel bristled. Not just at the words Cedric's friend, Lord Nigel Witherington, spoke, but rather that he spoke them in front of Kathleen. He turned to his sister.

"Lady Christina, Miss Roberts' groom is here to protect you both, please ride on and Stalwood and I shall catch up in a few minutes." He caught Christina's gaze, and she nodded, agreeing readily. His twin was so much in tune with him.

Once they were out of earshot, he turned to Cedric's friend. "Witherington, I would ask you to never again speak in such a derogatory way about the holy state of matrimony again in front of my intended. Miss Roberts need not hear such vulgarity."

"Oh, come now man, it was merely jesting. The ladies all know we call it a leg-shackle."

"That is as may be. But it is an arranged marriage. I do not want her to think I am not happy to marry her."

"Since when were you so keen to give up whores and gambling and be home as soon as the *Ton* entertainments were over."

"When my father asked me to marry."

"But no one sticks to their vows."

"I will," Gabriel announced with more fervour than necessary.

"I see. Will we see you tonight?"

"We shall be at the Barton ball."

"Fine." Cedric's friend nodded. "You seem different Onslow. More serious. Do not lose your sense of fun because you are trying to please the Duke. He shall die and you shall end up with nothing."

That made Gabriel stop and consider the words. Surely Cedric and Godfrey would be cared for in their father's will.

"My father will provide for me."

"Do not be so sure, Cede. These are hard times. The past couple of years have taken their toll. Why do you think your father is going into the iron trade with Miss Robert's father? Farming does not bring in the money it used to. You might find that the Duke leaves all his money to the Earl of Cindermaine, no matter how poorly he is."

His father surely would not leave Cedric and Godfrey penniless, would he? He liked the two sons he had sired to his mistress—probably even loved them in his own way. That said, his father was an ornery bugger and would do as he pleased. Who knew what sins Cedric might have committed in his eyes over the years and how the Duke would exact revenge in the long-term? In that moment, Gabriel realised that he didn't hate his brothers. None of what happened was their fault. Of course, Cedric was an ass. But he had been brought up that way. He had been spoiled and knew no different. Because he was the son of a Duke, albeit a bastard, the *Ton* kow-towed to him. No one would tell him he looked ridiculous. No one would tell him his behaviour was appalling. No one except his father, and his father wanted to keep Lady Benwick onside so she would continue to service him in the bedroom.

"I have every faith in my father, and if not, in my brother Gabriel. He is a good sort."

"No one has seen him."

"I have. I know he is kind."

"Well, as long as you know you will not have to change your lifestyle."

"Some things may have to change but it will all be for the good. Now I must go. The ladies are waiting. Good day, gentlemen."

He bowed in his saddle. Bowing was not a problem to him. He did it often as a servant. And as someone who was playing a mere gentleman, he was subordinate to two lords, even if they were the second son of an earl and third son of a marquis.

He turned his horse and nodded in Stalwood's direction. No words were needed. The two men trotted off in silence until they were out of earshot of Cedric's friends.

"So, Cedric has every faith in Gabriel. I'm sure Cedric would be surprised to hear that."

"I am not my father. Just because he might see my half-brothers penniless and homeless, does not mean I will. They are feckless asses. Of that, I have no doubt, but they have no role model. I hear from servants that their stepfather tried to instil discipline when they visited him, but the problem was that my father had already given them a home with us. My father pandered to them. And because he couldn't send them to school, they didn't have common sense knocked into them by their peers as we did."

"I see. So, you feel sorry for him."

"I feel sorry for them both, but the money will come at a price. He must treat Kathleen well. He must behave like a gentleman. No courtesans, no running up huge gambling debts and no more inexpressibles. I don't care how he wears his cravat, quite frankly. I do not want to see his prick and ballocks through his clothing."

Stalwood chuckled. "Thank the good Lord for that."

"Come, let us hurry and catch the ladies, but tell me, you and Christina, is it serious?"

"I have only known her a few days, but she intrigues me. She is not like other ladies of the *Ton*. She has a spark and a sharp wit. I could easily fall in love with her. And my concern is that your father may not wish her to marry a mere viscount if she were ever to consider me suitable."

"My father does not give two whits what happens to Christina. He is just upset she is not male. If she was, he could have seen to my demise and she, or rather, he could have inherited everything. Perhaps that is why he hates me so. I ruined his chances to have his spare."

"I don't understand ..." Stalwood started.

"Never mind," Gabriel waved him away.

Stalwood dropped it. "I still do not understand what he expects to achieve and how he expects it to play out once he dies. You suddenly make a miraculous recovery and take your place as the Duke?"

"I think he cares not. That shall be my problem and I shall have to explain it to the *Ton*. It will be a scandal, I am sure. And if I am old, I shall marry a young bride who shall provide me with an heir.

He does not care if I am happy or find love like he found with Lady Benwick all these years."

"You can still have companionship with your wife. I had it with mine, even though I feel more for your sister after a few days than I did for my wife after two years. Please do not misunderstand me. I cared deeply for her. I just did not have that attraction to her."

"And in bed?"

"She was a warm, willing body. An eager student as it were. I had no complaints."

"But would you have remained faithful to her?"

He sighed. "I must say, towards the end of her confinement, my eye was already straying. Of course, I had not acted on it, but I wanted to and it made me loathe myself."

"What proof do I have that you shall not be unfaithful to my sister?"

He smiled, his eyes glinting. They were approaching the ladies now. "I could never imagine wanting another woman if I had Christina in my bed. No woman compares to her. Why would you eat dry bread if you had pheasant on your table?"

Gabriel turned up his nose. "I hope that is not a euphemism, friend."

Stalwood chuckled. "It was not but now you mention it, I do like it as a euphemism."

"Uh, I wish to cast up my accounts."

"Please resist, otherwise Miss Roberts will worry that Cedric is ill again."

"I'll do my best."

The ladies had stopped their mounts and were waiting for them atop a slight rise. Gabriel's heart stuttered at Kathleen's beauty as she sat on her horse, tendrils of golden hair which had escaped her coiffeur fluttering in the breeze. His nether regions stirred, and he wriggled in his saddle. Devil take it. This was his half-brother's bride-to-be. He could not allow himself to develop tender feelings for her. Or worse—lustful feelings.

"And what about you and Miss Roberts?"

"What about me and Miss Roberts?" Gabriel asked scowling.

"You like her."

"She is pleasant."

"She is more than pleasant. I see how you cast your eyes over her, Gabe. You look like you want to devour her."

"I am pretending to be Cedric. That is how he would look at her."

"Of course." Stalwood gave him a sceptical eye-roll and Gabriel laughed. He had not fooled his friend.

"It matters not if I like her, Stalwood. She's Cedric's."

Stalwood drew Thunder to a halt and Gabriel did likewise.

"If you like her, and I mean really like her, we can do something. She should not have to marry that dandy of a half-brother of yours."

Gabriel shook his head. "Good Lord, Myles, has Thunder thrown you onto your head. It cannot happen. She is the betrothed of my bastard brother and that is the end of it." And with that, Gabriel dug his heels into the side of his horse. The animal took off towards the ladies, leaving Stalwood to catch him once he had gathered his wits.

Chapter 8

It had been ten days since her betrothal ball and all of Kathleen's initial worries about Cedric were in the past. He still had moments when he seemed a little offhand or supercilious—usually around other people, but Kathleen had concluded that deep down, Cedric was just a little shy. He used his façade to cover up his insecurities. Which was silly because he was charming and handsome and delightful company.

She had become fast friends with his half-sister Christina, who made sure they went to the same entertainments and always met up, often with the gentlemen. Kathleen knew Christina was falling in love with Lord Stalwood. But when Kathleen asked Christina about it, Christina waved her hand and said "Oh, he is a man of the world. What would he want with a spinster like me?"

It seemed to Kathleen that there was much to love about Christina. She was smart and funny and beautiful.

They were at afternoon tea at Lady Beaumont's and Cedric had led Kathleen into the conservatory to see the flowers.

While they were out of earshot of anyone else, they were still in view of everyone else. They could not sneak away for time alone at such a gathering. In fact, they had not been alone since the night of their betrothal ball and Kathleen felt as if Cedric's kiss had just been a dream.

"I heard some of the older ladies gossiping," Kathleen started. This was true. She had been privy to disturbing information and wanted to ask Cedric about it. She wanted to know about his relationship with a member of his family.

"You should not listen to gossip, Kathleen. Little of it is true."

"Mayhap. It was about Lord Byron."

He raised an eyebrow and looked at her. "Lord Byron."

"Yes. The poet."

"I know who he is and about his reputation."

"He has a half-sister."

"I am aware."

Heat rose in Kathleen's cheeks. "The gossiping ladies said he had ... well ..." She looked out over the flowerbeds. Anywhere but at Cedric. "They said he had intimate relations with his half-sister."

"That is one rumour about Byron, though not the most salacious and not the reason he lives in Switzerland."

"Oh?" She looked at him and his mouth quirked at the corner.

"I am not explaining why he is exiled, my love. That is for a time when you are much less innocent."

Kathleen bit her lip unsure how to ask what she wanted to know. "You and your half-sister are close."

Cedric coughed. "Good God, Kathleen. What are you implying? I love my sister. We're close but we are definitely not as close as Byron and his sister."

"So, you have never ..." Her voice trailed off. Cedric looked her straight in the eye.

"Never. I have never had the desire. The thought makes me feel quite ill. I am sure she is beautiful and lovely but not to me. Not in that way."

Kathleen smiled. "I am glad. After I heard those women talking, I wondered why Christina had not married."

"Christina is a little too forthright for her own good. She needs a man who shall not be intimidated by a woman who knows her own mind."

"A gentleman like Lord Stalwood."

"It seems that way."

"Perhaps we should encourage them. Christina likes him."

"They do not need encouraged, my love. Myles is making Christina fall head over ears in love with him without our help."

"And what will your father say?"

"I doubt my father cares who Christina marries, as long as he has a title and does not come back to my father looking for more money to keep her."

"Oh."

Cedric chuckled. "Do not look so distressed, Miss Roberts. It is the way of the *Ton*. Twas ever thus."

"And you? Why are you not marrying a young lady with a title?"

Cedric stopped and looked at her, assessing her. "I have no title to offer in return. But, having met you, and come to know you, if I had one, I would be honoured to give mine to you."

Heat rose in Kathleen's cheeks as Cedric suddenly started to inspect the flowers. He was embarrassed by his tender words. Somehow that just made her like him more.

"My father has a box at the theatre. If you have no plans tonight, perhaps I could get a party together and go," he said.

"I would enjoy that."

"Fine. I shall come around and pick you up in our carriage. I shall have Christina and Myles with me, so you shan't need a chaperone."

"Very well."

∞   ∞   ∞

"Why the devil are we going to Brooks's. My Father is not happy that I am gadding about as he puts it." Gabriel was less than happy.

"Keep a rein on that horse of yours, old chap, and all shall be revealed."

"Cedric would never be caught dead in Brooks's. Can you imagine that arse thinking paupers and women should get the vote? Come on, Myles. Should we not be keeping this farce at least in the realms of believability?"

"Gabe, my man, I swear I shall tell the whole of London who you are if you do not shut up. Either that or I shall tell them that Cedric is a molly and fancies someone in Brooks's."

"I would plant you a facer if you did."

"Remember what happened last time."

"But I am dressed as a gentleman tonight."

105

"We are here. Gabriel, try to pretend you are not in leading strings and trust me for once."

Gabriel rolled his eyes.

"Once my father pops off the mortal coil and I become a duke, I shall kill you Stalwood."

"Even dukes do not get away with murder, Cindermaine."

"Would you like to test that theory?"

"I would never know if it was true. I would be dead."

Damn Stalwood and his logic. He had always been able to out-argue him.

They walked into the club and the butler bowed to them.

"Viscount Stalwood and Mr Cedric Onslow to see Viscount Beattie."

Viscount Beattie? Gideon Beattie?

"Very good, My Lord."

The butler took their cloaks, hats, and canes, and then took them into the dining room. Several heads turned to face them, a couple of eyebrows raised, mainly in Gabriel's direction. He put on his best supercilious sneer and followed Stalwood. What the devil was his friend up to?

They were led to a dark corner of the dining room and Gabriel recognised his old school chum. He had not changed much. Stronger and bigger perhaps, but essentially the same.

"Thank you for meeting us, Beattie. I am sure you would rather be dining with your viscountess this evening."

"She is content with her aunt, as long as I do not make a habit of leaving her. Rumour has it, Stalwood that you shall have your own viscountess soon enough, and with Cindermaine's twin sister."

Beattie had looked right at him when he had said *Cindermaine,* and Gabriel suddenly felt his neck-cloth terribly restrictive. He tugged at it. Beattie held out his hand. Gabriel grasped it but rather than shake it, Beattie pulled him closer and spoke in a whisper. "Nice to see you again, Gabriel. Have a seat."

Gabriel sat, unable to think of anything to say. The footman brought wine and the gentlemen ordered and then they were alone. All the time they were ordering, Gabriel could only think of one thing—the one and only time he'd had to stand up to his father. The time he had planted him a facer and left him bleeding on the floor of his library. But he had never hit Christina again.

Did everyone know? If they did, it was a problem. His sire could lose his only reason to not hurt Christina. The combination of the secret being kept, Gabriel's obedience, and the threat he would kill his father, had kept his father from being violent to Christina for years. But if that man saw that his perfect world was beginning to fall like a barn with woodworm, he may just turn nasty again.

"Who knows?" he said eventually.

"Who knows what?"

Gabriel glanced behind him and around the room to check no one would overhear. He spoke through his teeth in undertones. "Who knows I am Cindermaine, damn it."

Stalwood flinched. "Only your household staff, Christina, and Beattie."

"My wife knows too."

"Oh God, well if Lady Clumsy knows, the whole of the *Ton* knows."

Beattie rose to his feet.

"Gideon, he does not mean it. Please," Stalwood said, laying a hand on Beattie's arm.

Gabriel ran his hand through his hair. "I apologise unreservedly. That was uncalled for. Please, Beattie, accept my humblest of apologies. Your dear wife does not deserve to be the butt of my bad temper."

Beattie stood for a moment then looked at Stalwood. "What the hell happened to him."

Stalwood shrugged. "He refuses to tell me all that happened. Something to do with his mother when he was a child. Before he even went to Eton. Christina refuses to tell me as she refuses to betray his confidence. I tried everything with her."

"You had better not have bedded her." Gabriel knew he was being unreasonable. He knew he was being an arse. But he could not help himself. What if others had worked it out?

"Are you sure you brought Cindermaine and not Onslow?"

"Yes, I can tell them apart. Though for most of the *Ton* they just look at the nose and the hair. You see, the eyes and the mouth differentiate who is who. Granted, it is difficult with this one permanently scowling."

"Are we done?"

"No." Both his old school friends said together.

"Why am I here?"

"Well, Gideon does not know why you, or indeed he, is here. But Christina and I hatched a plan. And we decided to be your fairy godmothers."

"You mean like in a children's tale?"

"Indeed."

"What the devil?"

"Well, Cindermaine, Christina and I think you should go to the ball, or in this case, the wedding."

"I do not understand." He looked from Stalwood—who looked excited and pleased with his cunning plan—to Beattie, who looked as perplexed as he felt.

"You are developing tender feelings for Miss Roberts. Yes?"

Gabriel scowled. If truth be known, he could not get the adorable chit out of his mind. Today she had been wearing a light blue gown which was low cut and high-waisted. She had worn a dainty string of pearls around her delicate neck—a neck he was desperate to kiss. When her cheeks had turned pink as she had asked if he'd had inappropriate relations with Christina, he'd had quite scandalous thoughts about her. His breeches were getting tight at the thought of her.

Beattie lifted an eyebrow at Stalwood. "I believe we have our answer to that question if the starry expression on his face is anything to go by."

"Oh, shut up. I have no starry expression on my face, Beattie."

"If you say so."

"So, the idea of Cedric's hands all over her naked body and coupling with her ..."

Gabriel let out a low growl at Stalwood who raised two hands in surrender. "You must marry the chit, old boy, or that will become the reality." It was Beattie's voice cutting through the red haze of rage.

Marry her.

Then Cedric won't have her.
Make her yours.
You care for her.
It makes sense.

They were all just words. Gabriel shook his head as their dinner was served. It gave him time to gather his wits a little.

"So, I just march into Hartsmere House and announce I am marrying my brother's betrothed, I suppose," he said, with an added edge of sarcasm.

"Hardly. I suppose the first thing you must do is tell Miss Roberts and swear her to secrecy."

"You realise that this sort of scandal ruins young ladies," Gabriel pointed out.

"True," said Beattie, "But unless your father outlives you, she shall be a duchess and duchesses rise above scandal. And even if you meet an untimely demise, she will be a dowager countess, which will stand her in good stead."

"And let us be honest, chaps. Cedric will bring scandal on her, no matter what. He is not the soul of discretion, is he?" pointed out Stalwood.

"All good points, gentlemen. But I have no money and my father will disown me. What are we to live on?"

"Her dowry?" suggested Beattie

"That is her money."

"I shall give you money until you come into your inheritance, Gabe." It was Stalwood. It was a very tempting offer but not one that Gabriel could contemplate. "No."

"Christina has offered you her dowry once we wed. She said she owes it to you. I have not asked more. We have no need for it, and I will care for my wife and make sure she is provided for in the event of my death," Stalwood persisted.

"I cannot take money from my own sister."

"She is insistent."

God's teeth. Did the man think he had no pride? Gabriel scowled at his best friend.

"Why are you discussing this with Christina?" He swallowed hard, trying to rein in his temper. He had not been angry for years. For so long he had just accepted what had come his way. And now it felt as if Stalwood was poking him with a stick and this sleeping wild animal did not want to be disturbed.

"It was her idea. Whether you like it or not, Cindermaine, your sister loves you and wants you to be happy and I love her, and I want her to be happy. And she will not marry me until she knows you are out of that house and away from that man."

"I do not need my sister's protection," Gabriel said through gritted teeth.

"She is not offering you protection, My Lord. She is offering you money to marry the woman for whom you have tender feelings. Then you can become the man you are supposed to be rather than a god-damned servant."

"Wait, a servant?" Beattie's eyes were wide and his jaw slack.

"You did not tell him?" Gabriel asked looking between the men.

"No, Gabriel. I did not tell him. When I saw him at the betrothal ball, I asked if we could meet here. I thought here was better than White's or Tattersall's. But I did not get the opportunity to meet up before and explain what I knew. Gideon recognised you at the ball. We were friends at Eton. He, like me, could tell the difference. He spoke to me rather than you because you were busy that night. I believe you were entertaining Miss Roberts in the hothouse at that point."

Gabriel had a growing sense of unease. He had not thought through his impulsive visit to the conservatory with Miss Roberts. Had everyone noticed? But then nearly everyone thought he was Cedric.

"Tell me what? What is this about you being a servant? Were you not ill and at the Hartsmere estate? What the devil is going on Cindermaine?"

Gabriel glowered at Stalwood for a moment, but the time had come to be honest. As much as he could be.

"I was never ill. Well, apart from the odd fever. Nothing serious. When I was five, something happened and, because of my actions, my mother …" He took a deep breath. "My mother took her own life."

"Christ." It was Myles. Gabriel felt cold and sick. He pushed his chair out slightly and looked at his evening shoes as he laid down his knife and fork. But when he chanced a glance at Beattie, the man looked unperturbed.

"My father killed himself," said Beattie in hushed tones. "We lied to the vicar. Told him the doctor said it was his heart. I could not have my sister Sophia go through any more pain and the scandal of him being buried at a crossroads." Beattie stuck his chin out. "Well … I know it's a sin, but I do not care. Anyway, what terrible deed can a five-year-old do that can cause a woman to take her own life. Did you not wash behind your ears properly?"

Gabriel gave a humourless chuckle. That was so like Gideon to ask such a ridiculous question. Could he tell the whole truth to his friends?

Well, he'd come this far.

"I was playing near the dower house one day when I was about five," Gabriel started, toying with the stem of his port glass.

"Cedric and Godfrey had already come to live with us. Mother had accepted them to a degree and believed my father had stopped his affair with their mother. Lady Benwick had not yet married Baron Benwick. She married him not long after though, as I recall. Anyway, I passed by a French window that led into one of the sitting rooms in the dower house, and my father had a lady bent over a loveseat. He was smacking her bottom and pulling her hair. He was also pumping his cock in and out of her, hard and fast."

"Good God. In broad daylight, while you were playing close by?" asked Stalwood.

"He likely did not know I was outside. I should have been in the care of a nurse, but I had a bad habit of escaping her watchful eye. She was elderly and occasionally dozed off. Anyway, I had no idea about sex. I was only five. It appeared to my five-year-old self that my father was hurting her. He had given me a few thumps in my time. I knew my mama had been given the odd bruise at his hand. Even Christina."

"Christina!" Myles spoke with a growl through his teeth. "You did not mention that the day we rode in Hyde Park."

"No, well, he does not hit her now. I saw to that when I was old enough to fight back. However, back when I was five, I was worried for the lady my sire was tumbling. I did not know her, or that she was Cedric and Godfrey's mother."

Gabriel raked his fingers though his hair. "So, I went to my own mother and recounted what I had seen. Of course, my mama put two and two together. Godfrey is younger than Christina and me, so she knew when he was born that the affair was not over. But the Duke had promised her after Godfrey it was ended. She did not believe she had a love match, but mayhap she had hoped she had a foundation on which to build. To be honest, as an adult, I do not understand how she could be so naïve about the man."

"What happened then?" asked Beattie, pulling him away from his introspection.

"Marchby is an old castle. It has turrets which are six storeys high. She climbed to the top of one of them the next night after a confrontation with my sire and threw herself off one of the battlements. She was found the next morning by a maid going out to get milk. My father beat me black and blue."

"But when you were old enough, he sent you to Eton."

"I will be the Duke of Hartsmere one day. I had to get my education. But you may have noticed that I always returned to the Hartsmere estate in the holidays, and no one ever visited Hartsmere with me."

"That is true," Stalwood said.

"I worked with the men on the estate and once I left university, I was given a uniform and I became a footman. I often help my friend with jobs that pertain to being Cedric's valet because he is such a fussy bugger. Cochrane could not do it all himself. It takes him half an hour to do the man's neckcloth in that intricate knot. So, I polish his boots and mend his clothes and de-flea them after he has been in the most disreputable of brothels."

"And this is why Cedric is suddenly wearing silk evening breeches instead of inexpressibles?"

"Would you wear anything that had been near Cedric's ballocks?" Gabriel asked, an eyebrow raised.

Both his companions made faces that showed their distaste. "I think you just put me off my port, my dear man," said Stalwood.

"Imagine having to mend his inexpressibles. Cochrane and I have wagers to see who must do it. Cochrane usually loses."

"Well, it seems even more clear now that this cannot go on," said Stalwood.

"It is my punishment for having a big mouth and poking my nose in where I should not, as the Duke says."

"You were a child. Barely out of leading-strings," said Beattie. "No, this isn't acceptable. You are Cindermaine. Your title may only be courtesy now, but you are still a lord. And you care for that chit. She cannot be forced to marry that arse who shows his prick off to the world, even if it is covered by a thin layer of fabric."

"Christ, Beattie, please do not make me think about Cedric's prick. I shall cast up my accounts," moaned Stalwood

"First things first, you need to tell the lady and then you shall have to procure a special licence. Beat Cedric to the chase, as it were," said Beattie, sitting back and folding his arms across his chest as if it were easy.

"I still have no money," Gabriel protested.

"You will pay us back when you get your inheritance. And if you die before your father, well, we shall be glad to have helped a friend who had a very short life," said Stalwood, his voice soothing as though he were speaking to his damned horse.

"He could live until he is ninety."

"Oh we shall see to it that you invest your money wisely and then you shall not be living off us for long," Beattie assured him. "I invested most of my money my father gave me from when I attended university and damned good thing too. He wagered the rest away. We shall, thanks to my wife's dowry, survive this past dreadful year."

"I do not think I can agree to that, gentlemen." Gabriel loved that his friends were so concerned but he had his pride.

"You have to, if not for your own sake, then for the sake of Miss Roberts. Would you really leave her to marry Cedric?" Stalwood raised an eyebrow at him.

"Devil take it, Myles. He is not nice to women. The maids all say he is not exactly ... well, he does not force them, but he never leaves them alone until they give in to his whining demands. Then he is rough with them. And I mean ... not in the way a lady likes one to get a little ... you know."

"You mean not an erotic slap on the bottom and not her agreeing to be tied to the bedpost while you pleasure her," said Stalwood knowingly. Well it was good to know he wasn't the only one.

"Quite. He borders on cruel from what they tell me."

"Rumour has it, he is banned from the brothels where you find a better class of courtesan because of his treatment of the ladies. Really, Gabriel, this young lady cannot be subjected to this."

"Some young lady shall," Gabriel said morosely.

"We shall cross the bridge of the next young lady when needs must. Let us deal with you and Miss Roberts now. Besides, you have a tendre for her."

Yes, he did.

"It shall not work." He shook his head.

"We shall make it work. You can live in my bloody dower house if necessary. But with luck, your father will not stop you living in Marchby House or Marchby Castle. It is your birth right. Once the truth of your good health is out there, hopefully, he shall want to save face."

"So, I must tell Miss Roberts the truth. And get her to agree to marry me instead of Cedric."

"It should be simple enough," said Stalwood. "Christina assures me she is already halfway in love with you."

"Let us go our separate ways and collect our ladies and take them to the theatre. You can tell her on the way home."

"Perhaps. Or I may tell her tomorrow. Take her for a walk. I shall think about it at the theatre."

Chapter 9

Cedric was quiet and distracted that evening, but he had not once affected that air of fashionable ennui he sometimes put on in front of others. They were using his father's box, and he had brought along Lord Stalwood and Lady Christina. Viscount and Viscountess Beattie, whom Kathleen thought she may have met at her betrothal ball, had also been invited. But she had met so many people that evening it was hard to remember.

Lady Beattie was lovely and sweet and asked her to accompany her to the necessary. Lady Beattie had just found out she was increasing and needed to visit the necessary more than usual. She had apologised for her brutal honesty but had said she usually found it easier just to state the obvious. While Kathleen was not used to this direct approach, she found it refreshing.

They were just arriving back at their box when an elderly woman approached Lady Beattie.

"Emily, my dear, how are you?"

"I am fine, Aunt." Lady Beattie introduced Kathleen to Lady Wardlaw, her aunt, and they exchanged a few pleasantries before her aunt started to tell her a long-winded story. Raised voices from their box, however, caught Kathleen's attention.

"I will tell her in my own good time, Christina. I cannot just blurt out that I am not Cedric, but in fact, his half-brother, the heir to the Dukedom of Hartsmere. Nor that she only met Cedric once, on the day he cast up his accounts outside her house."

"Be quiet. She could be back at any moment." It was Christina's voice.

"How will she react? And furthermore, I have to tell her we suspect he might be a bit of a brute to women, and she should marry me. Which is all well and good, but we have no idea if we may have to live in poverty for anything up to fifty years should the Duke live to a ripe old age."

"You shall not live in poverty. We have discussed this. We shall make sure you are comfortable, Cindermaine. Cedric lives off your father. I do not see the difference, Gabriel." That sounded like Lord Stalwood.

"There is a big difference. We lied to her. The Duke may have been the instigator of the lie, but we went along with it."

"She would be miserable with Cedric. I cannot bear to be in his company for even a few minutes far less a lifetime."

"I know, and I understand. I agree with you all. But I have to do this in my own time."

"You have no time, Gabriel. Cedric is regaining his strength. Gentlemen are supposed to be honourable. Kathleen is my friend. You would make a good match. I know you have an affection for her. You must marry her and soon."

"I do apologise." Lady Beattie was smiling at her as the elderly lady walked away leaning heavily on a cane. "Once Aunt Gertrude gets a bee in her bonnet about something there is no stopping her. Honestly, you would think it the crime of the century that Lady Parker forgot to add milk to her teacup before adding the tea. Come, we shall be late for the start of the next act."

Kathleen's mind was in a whirl. Cedric was not Cedric. He was Gabriel, the half-brother who was supposed to be ill and in the country. And they thought Cedric might be a brute, but they were not sure. But they had all lied to her. Now they wanted her to marry Gabriel. But he would be poor. How could the son of a Duke be poor? The Duke was making a grand investment in papa's company. It was all very confusing.

Gabriel was smiling at her as she and Lady Beattie re-entered the box. She sat down giving him a wan smile.

"Are you enjoying the play?" he asked.

"I am not so keen on Shakespeare's tragedies, I must confess," she replied. If she was honest, she was more intrigued by the drama unfolding in this box.

"Nor I, Miss Roberts."

"Miss Roberts?"

"We must be formal in case opera glasses and lorgnettes are trained on us and those watching can read our lips."

She raised her fan to her face and opened it.

"Were you not afraid of that during the interval, Lord Cindermaine?"

He turned his head towards her and his face visibly paled. Kathleen raised an eyebrow back at him.

"Kathleen, I ..."

But the actors were coming back on stage and everyone started to quieten down. She turned her face to the stage in a most definite cut. Thankfully he chose not to press her further.

Kathleen bit her lip and willed the burning behind her eyes to stop. She would not cry. She could not. Not in front of all these people. Every eye would be upon her if she broke down. She needed time to work out what was happening and what all this meant.

∞   ∞   ∞

Eventually, the play was over and Gabriel, as it appeared that he was called, handed her up into Lord Stalwood's carriage. He then climbed in himself after Christina and sat down. She wanted to move. She did not want to sit next to Lord Cindermaine. That said, she did not want to sit opposite him and look into those eyes. She had glanced at him a few times through the rest of the performance and his gaze had been lowered. She was sure he had worried a hole in the thumb of his evening glove. So much so that at one point, Christina, who sat on his other side had placed a hand on his and smiled sweetly at him. He had grimaced and she had glanced knowingly at Kathleen, then back at him and he had nodded. Could they communicate with their minds? She had heard some twins could do that.

The carriage horses moved off a couple of yards then stopped.

"It always takes some time to get out of the Drury Lane area. And I believe the Worthington's are also having a ball this evening. That will not help. But let us discuss the elephant in the carriage shall we?" said Lord Stalwood.

"Not now, Stalwood," Gabriel growled.

"If not now, then when?"

"Indeed," said Kathleen. "It is time I was told the truth. Would you not agree, Lord Cindermaine?"

"I agree," said Christina softly

"So, it was you I met at the ball? You in the hothouse?" Anger mixed with embarrassment made her cheeks flame at the thought. He had taken advantage of her.

"Yes, that was me."

"The one who accidentally called himself Gabriel, is that correct, Lord Cindermaine?"

"Why do you keep calling me by my title?"

"Cedric gave me leave to call him by his given name, you have not," she replied tartly.

"That was me. The last time you saw Cedric, he was casting up his accounts in front of your townhouse."

"Is he well?"

"He shall live. And I, Gabriel, Earl of Cindermaine give you leave to call me by my given name, Miss Roberts."

Chapter 15

Gabriel arrived at Gideon Beattie's townhouse in Audley Street in his servant's clothes, only for the butler to look at him with disdain.

"Gabriel Marchby to see Lord Beattie. He's expecting me."

"Lord Beattie is entertaining this evening, I'm afraid. He is not expecting any other visitors."

"He is expecting me. Did he say the Earl of Cindermaine was dining with him?"

"And what has that to do with you?"

"I am the Earl of Cindermaine."

"I hardly think so. If you could just ..."

"Lord Cindermaine. It is fine, Grantham. Lord Cindermaine is dining with us. Really Gabriel, why did you not change?" asked Gideon's sweet new wife.

"I could not very well walk out of the Duke's townhouse wearing aristocratic finery, could I, Lady Beattie?"

"Oh, call me Emily, please."

"Ma'am I can ..." started the butler.

"Find out when dinner will be ready, Grantham."

The butler nodded and headed to the back of the house. "He hates me," Emily confided in Gabriel.

"He does not yet know you. Servants seldom hate their employers unless they are cruel or mean."

"That is what I keep telling her." Gideon was walking along the hallway.

"He thinks I am clumsy."

"My darling, you are clumsy, but I love every clumsy bone in your body and I hated that china anyway."

"What if I drop the baby?"

He chuckled. "Not as likely with a baby than with a cup, my love."

"You are being silly, Emily. If I can manage with my legs, you can manage being a little clumsy." Gabriel glanced up to see the Duke of Kirkbourne carrying the Duchess up the hallway. "Assuming you live through this infernal need to visit the necessary, of course." She gave Emily a rueful smile.

"You have all this to come, gentlemen," said the Duke, nodding his head to Gabriel and Gideon. He stopped dead in his tracks and his gaze narrowed. "Cindermaine?"

"Yes. Pleased to meet you, Your Grace. Stalwood is bringing decent clothes for me to change into. I apologise for these ..." He brushed a hand down his coat.

"Never mind your coat. No wonder you were able to pull off the switch. You do look like Onslow. Though not so much around the eyes and mouth. And you are sturdier."

Gabriel curled his lips and affected fashionable ennui. "But Your Grace, I do such a good impersonation of my bastard half-brother." Kirkbourne barked out a laugh, and it was only then Gabriel remembered there were ladies in the room. "Oh, I do apologise. I should never have said that word with ladies present. Please, Your Grace, ladies, can you ever forgive me?"

"Oh my, Gabriel, Gideon says much worse, and I even got him to tell me why Lord Byron is exiled to the continent."

"Why are women obsessed by that?" Kirkbourne asked Gabriel.

"I have no idea. My sister and Kathleen have both asked me."

"I ended up explaining to Sarah. If for nothing else, to get me some peace."

"Have they asked you about mollies yet."

"No," said Gabriel.

"Yes," said Kirkbourne at the same time. Kirkbourne slapped him on the back. "More for you to look forward to. Once they discover the joys of the bedchamber, they want to learn about everything. Set her up with copies of *The School of Venus* and *Fanny Hill* and she should be quiet for a week."

"Are they not both banned books?"

"What the government does not know, the government does not cry over."

"As a peer of the realm, are you not the government?"

Kirkbourne made a gesture that suggested he was on the fence on that argument. "I shall procure your young lady copies since you are currently in a difficult spot."

"I shall be in a more difficult spot if either of us ends up in Newgate for reading banned books."

"I know a Duke who will pull strings to get you out. Never fear."

"As long as it is not the Duke of Hartsmere."

"Never him."

∞ ∞ ∞

Gabriel had never been to a formal dinner before, except at university and his betrothal ball. He felt out of his element. However, he knew Lady Beattie had arranged the seating in an unconventional manner—seating husbands and wives together. He suspected this was because she knew that Christina and Stalwood, and he and Kathleen were not being given the opportunity to spend time together at present. It was thoughtful and the Duke and Duchess did not seem to mind. She did, however, allow Kirkbourne to lead his wife into dinner first, as was expected since he had precedence as a duke.

While he enjoyed conversing with Kathleen and the Duchess on his other side about rather mundane topics, he half-wished that Lady Beattie had placed Kathleen and him on opposite sides of the table. Then the temptation to touch her would not be constant. Had he not consummated the marriage the day before, then he would have been less aware of the delights of her body. Oh of course, as a man he wanted her. Who would not? She was beautiful, had a wonderful figure, a glorious, sunny smile and glowing, peachy skin. It was why gentlemen took second looks at her. Well, he knew it was her décolletage they took second glances at. He was no fool.

He glanced at it now and felt himself harden. Devil take it.

"You are wool-gathering, My Lord," Kathleen whispered into his ear as she laid her hand on his silk evening breeches that Stalwood had brought for him to change into.

"I am thinking about you."

"What are you thinking about specifically?"

He glanced at the Duchess, who was deep in conversation with her husband. He moved her hand up his breeches so that, for the briefest moment she touched his hard length through the material. Her eyes widened.

"I am thinking about how I would like to use that on you."

"My Lord."

He gave her a crooked smile.

"Do not ask questions, if you do not want a truthful answer."

"You are leading me astray, My Lord."

"One can only hope."

After dinner, the ladies retired to the drawing room for tea while the gentlemen remained in the dining room for port and cheroots.

"You realise my wife has prepared bedchambers for you both," Beattie said, pointing his lit cheroot at Stalwood and Gabriel.

"Why the devil did she do that?" Stalwood asked, laying his port on the table and sitting back.

"My wife is an incurable romantic. Especially in the matter of Cindermaine here. Every time he and his situation come up in conversation, her eyes become distinctly watery and she gives me a look that implores me to ameliorate the situation. As if I, a lowly viscount, have any power over a duke."

"I am receiving similar reproving looks from my wife," put in Kirkbourne. "And I am a duke, but what can I do?"

"Interesting as these tales of your wives are, what have they to do with the bedchambers being prepared?" asked Gabriel, still perplexed.

"Well, Emily is devastated that your wedding night did not happen, or rather it happened in an afternoon in an inn. She bemoans that it is desperately unromantic and that you should have a comfortable bed in a townhouse in Mayfair."

"This townhouse?"

"Indeed."

"When?"

"After dinner."

"So when you and Kirkbourne are entertaining your wives and ... what? Playing cards? Stalwood and I would be in your guest bedchambers tumbling our wives."

Beattie sighed and took a swig from his port. "I did not say it was one of her better ideas. I tried to talk her out of it."

"Can we just remember that Lady Stalwood is my sister and I have no desire to be in the bedchamber next to hers when Stalwood has her invoking the name of our saviour and lord. I shared a womb with the creature and have no wish to share anything more intimate with her."

"I am sure the feeling is mutual on her part," muttered Stalwood.

"No doubt."

Kirkbourne looked at Gabriel as he drew on his cheroot. "Tell me, Cindermaine, after the Christmas Season is past and Prinny returns to London, would you be annoyed at me if I spoke to him on your behalf?"

"And said what?" Gabriel raised an eyebrow in interest.

"To be honest, at present, I do not know. I wonder if he could give you your own title, separate from that of the Hartsmere Dukedom, that can merge with the Hartsmere title when you succeed to it." He paused for a moment, to let the idea sink in. Stalwood and Beattie were nodding their heads slowly as if it wasn't the most stupid idea they'd heard.

"I have no idea if it can be done or ever has been. And doubt very much if Prinny will know, but the man is a real bleeding heart with a truly romantic soul, rather like my wife but with a prick and ballocks. If there is a way to do it, your rather sad story is sure to tug at his heartstrings."

Gabriel screwed up his nose. "I do not want his pity."

"Oh, my dear fellow, we all have his pity. I have his pity because I am not a prince and therefore, in his eyes, not as lucky as he. Of course, I would not wish his life for all the tea in China. I am more than happy with my lot in life and understand that when the die was cast in life, I was one of the fortunate ones. You should have been one of the fortunate ones, but your sire is an arse."

"You say that, Kirkbourne, but you only take my word for it."

"I have had dealings with Hartsmere in the past and I see the state of his elder bye blow. I do not know Godfrey, if I am honest. But when I have come across him, he seems slightly more amenable than his brother."

"He is. He took me to buy clothing the day that the Duke decided I should impersonate Cedric at the ball for his betrothal. While in the Duke's study, he was ridiculous, but once alone in the carriage to Bond Street, he was pleasant, asking me to do my impersonation of Cedric which he found hilarious. He has even started wearing buckskin breeches and silk evening knee breeches instead of inexpressibles."

"He asked me the other day if I would mind awfully becoming his friend," said Stalwood.

Gabriel turned to Stalwood. "Really?"

"Indeed. I said I would be honoured but perhaps we should keep it to ourselves just now until things settle with Cedric's marriage. Just in case Miss Roberts works out that Gabriel is masquerading as Cedric."

"That was clever of you," said Beattie.

"Well, if I were truly honest, I am not opposed to being the lad's friend. He is Christina's half-sibling. And he shows promise of being a decent human being, unlike Cedric. Christina thinks he is afraid of Cedric and the Duke and is praying for the day the Duke pops off this mortal coil and leaves him the hell alone. She says he is sometimes nice to her and occasionally seeks out her company when no one else is in the house."

"She has never said anything to me about it," Gabriel said, frowning.

"I believe she still considers him the enemy and worries you shall think she is disloyal to you. You know she thinks the world of you Gabe and would walk across fire for you, do you not?"

"As I would for her. I could never think Christina disloyal. She can be a silly goose."

"Well, for so long, she was your only ally in the aristocracy. She knew you had good friends among the staff, but it was a heavy burden. It is part of the reason she did not try harder to find a husband."

"Well, it is all coming out now, is it not?" mused Gabriel. "We should sell this story to a playwright and let them make it into a drawing room farce to be shown at Drury Lane. Though it is all so far-fetched, I am not sure anyone would believe it. Perhaps it could be made into one of those gothic novels that Christina is so keen on."

"Byron could write poetry about you," put in Kirkbourne, chuckling.

"Do not mention bloody Byron. I have had enough questions about that man to last a lifetime," said Beattie. Everyone nodded in agreement.

"Did you tell your wife why he is in exile?" Gabriel asked, looking at Beattie.

"I had to. Before we wed, I said I would tell her once she was no longer an innocent, thinking it meant she would forget. Of course, the horses had turned onto the highway from her brother's estate, but I doubt the carriage even had when she was demanding I explain. So I did."

"Devil take it. Do you think all the married ladies in the *Ton* know why he was exiled?"

"Probably. They're such gossips. Unless their husbands are such prudes, they shall not tell them."

"Well, I can only hope your wife explains it to mine, thus relieving me of the duty," said Gabriel.

Beattie chuckled. "I swore her to secrecy. You married her. She is your responsibility now. Even if only to explain salacious gossip to her." Gabriel grimaced.

"At least once Christmas Day is over, I shall have other more pleasant marital tasks to perform."

"The bedchambers are at your disposal," said Beattie, waggling an eyebrow. Gabriel made a rude gesture at his friend and they all laughed. He lifted his port but glanced around his friends before taking a drink.

This should have been his life long before now instead of avoiding drunken bar brawls in taverns in St Giles. His birthright had been all but stolen because of something he had done as a small child. Resentment roiled in his belly. Resentment towards his sire, his half-brothers, his sire's mistress and yes, even towards his mother for her selfish actions. For leaving two five-year-old children to the wrath of the monster that was the Duke of Hartsmere.

"He's wool-gathering. I suspect he has that bedchamber in mind, Beattie." It was Stalwood. Gabriel smiled and forced a chuckle. Better they think he was thinking of tumbling his pretty wife than they know of the dark and brooding turn his thoughts had taken.

Nothing more was said about the bedchambers and Gabriel was glad of it. Tempting though it was, he found it all rather gauche. He did not want everyone to think he was so desperate for sex, he would remove his wife from company to take her to bed, even if it was exactly what he wanted to do.

At the end of the evening, he changed back into his servant's clothes and climbed atop Stalwood's carriage with the driver. Stalwood handed the ladies inside the carriage and Gabriel tipped his cap to Beattie who had come out onto the street as the carriage took off.

Gabriel was surprised then when, as they arrived at Kathleen's house, the driver steered the horses around towards the mews. When the coach stopped Stalwood helped Kathleen out then gestured him down. He jumped off the box and raised an eyebrow at his friend.

"Lady Cindermaine wanted time in private with you," said Stalwood with a conspiratorial wink.

"I see."

"I can go in the back door. I shall think of a suitable excuse. Perhaps we can rip my gown or something." Kathleen's voice was breathy.

"You want me to rip your gown."

"It would be a good excuse, would it not?" She bit her lip and he softened his tone.

"Maybe."

Kathleen rolled her eyes. "Come into the garden. Lord Stalwood, as ever, thank you."

He bowed his head to her. "Lady Cindermaine, the pleasure is all mine. Cindermaine." He bowed his head and Gabriel bowed back too.

"Stalwood." This felt terribly stuffy. "Myles. Thank you."

Myles grinned. "You know where I am, Gabe."

"I do."

"Is that not what you say to me," said Kathleen, giggling.

"I believe, I already have, my love."

She led him in the gate and as soon as it was shut, she pulled him a little way up the dark path before she twirled and cupped his face, kissing him. He could do nothing but wrap his arms around her and kiss her back. Despite the cold, he was immediately aroused, especially when his pretty little wife unfastened the buttons of his breeches and began to stroke him.

"Kathleen. What are you doing?" he asked as he unfastened the top button of her pelisse, trying to find some skin that he could kiss.

"Emily wanted us to use one of her bedchambers, but it felt … wrong. But Gabriel, I know you do not want to do it the way your … the Duke did it, but it is me and I lo—care for you. It is not wrong. Please. I can brace my hands on the bench there."

"It is wrong to make love in our friend's bedchamber but it is fine for me to tup you like an animal in your back garden in the freezing cold, Kathleen."

"That is why you must hurry. I was thinking about it this afternoon. That is why I asked Lord Stalwood to have the carriage brought round to the mews. It was also why I am so wet where you … where we … well, I keep thinking about it and it is very invigorating."

"Oh God. Are you telling me you are aroused?"

"I believe I am." He found the skin on her neck and pressed his lips to it. Kathleen sighed and gripped his prick harder.

"If you end up with an ague, it is entirely your own fault," he argued without conviction. Why was he even contemplating this? It was freezing.

"Please Gabriel. It is so very hard being married and yet not being with you."

"It is certainly hard, my love. Devil take it but I have no self-control with you."

He whirled her around towards the bench, placed her hands on it and lifted her skirts and pelisse. He moved his fingers around the hem of the skirt until he found the seam then grasped it in both hands. It took a few tries because the garment was so well made but eventually the seam gave way and he ripped a large tear in it.

He needed to be quick. It was far too cold for this type of activity, and he was a brute for letting her talk him into it. He took his prick in hand and rubbed it through her wet folds. She had not been exaggerating. She was wet. She moaned quietly. She was very aroused, and it made his heart sing. He pushed into her and when he was halfway in, she pushed back, impaling herself fully on him. She was so eager and needed no tutoring. Every movement came naturally to her.

He moved one hand around her hips so that he could tease her pearl as he thrust into her hard and fast, hoping the friction would bring her to orgasm quickly.

When she rested her head on her forearm on the bench, he was ready to stop, but her moan of "Gabriel, that is so good," spurred him on. And when her other hand moved over his to urge him to increase the pressure on her nub, Gabriel thought he might release before her, right there, like a callow youth.

"Move your legs together, Kathleen," he said, and she obeyed, increasing the friction and changing the angle. She threw back her head on a moan of pleasure. "Let go, my love," he urged as he increased his pace. He was anything but cold now. His release was imminent. He was just losing his rhythm when his wife's body pulsed around his prick.

"Oh my. Oh Gabe. Oh. Oh help. Oh my."

He grabbed for the bench back as he drove into her, releasing his seed in what felt like an unending stream. The waves of pleasure almost turning him mindless. He did, however, have the presence of mind to grab Kathleen around the waist and keep her upright.

As he came back to himself, he stood with Kathleen plastered against his body. They were already separated. She turned in his embrace and wrapped her arms around him as if he was a piece of driftwood she was clinging to in a stormy sea.

"I should have withdrawn from your body to release my seed. I am sorry," was all he could manage.

"No, I like the feel of it."

"I have a handkerchief to clean the worst of it."

"I shall be going straight to my bedchamber."

"You need to get inside, Kathleen. It is far too cold."

"Do I get a goodnight kiss."

"Indeed you do."

He bent his head and put every ounce of passion and feeling into the kiss. This woman had become his driftwood, and he did not like the fact he had to be separated from her anymore. And it had little to do with sex, though that was indeed extremely pleasant. But he feared what might happen if the Duke and Cedric found out their secret before they were ready.

Chapter 16

When a note arrived for Kathleen the next day, she was sitting in the parlour reading. The butler entered the room with the piece of paper on a silver salver. She thanked him and opened it, wondering who it could be from.

My Dearest Miss Roberts,

Thank you for being my dinner companion last evening. The night took an interesting turn right at the end. It was most enjoyable. While I should very much like to repeat the experience, I fear it is not wise given the weather. However, since I am unable to see you today or this evening, I shall be where the event happened last evening at midnight tonight, should you wish to attend a short meeting.

Please destroy this note immediately so that it is not found. Your fiancé is expected at the same entertainment as you this evening. Please take care. I only wish to check that you are well and see it with my own eyes.

Yours ever.

GM

He would be at the bench at midnight. She would most definitely be there. Kathleen knew he was concerned for her safety given Cedric's behaviour the other night, but she had spoken to Emily, Sarah and Christina and they had arranged to all go to the same events during the run-up to Christmas day. She would stay close to her friends to avoid being alone with Cedric and prevent any nasty moments from happening.

When she arrived at the Langley ball, she sat down beside the Duchess. She had decided that dancing would not be on her itinerary this evening. However, The Duke, Lord Beattie and Lord Stalwood all added their names to her dance card. That, of course, was fine. When Cedric approached her to ask for a dance, she put him after the others. The Duke was the third gentleman on her card and when he came over with lemonade for her and his wife she spoke to him.

"Your Grace, I do beg your pardon, but at the end of our dance, would you mind awfully if I feign a turned ankle and you have to help me off the dance floor?"

"Trying to avoid someone?"

She grimaced. "Cedric wants to dance."

"Well, in that case, I'll be more than happy to oblige. Otherwise, I am happy to punch him in the face for you. Either would suffice."

Kathleen bit back a laugh. "No, Your Grace. A turned ankle shall be sufficient to deter him. A half hour in his company is more than I can bear."

"Well, I must consider myself honoured then that you shall wait until the end of the dance before you turn your ankle."

"Oh Nate, stop teasing the poor girl," put in Sarah. "You know fine you are a handsome, charming devil.

He raised an eyebrow at his wife.

"I recall you calling me a beast earlier."

"Well, you can be that too. You can be somewhat overbearing at times. It is that aristocratic air you have about you."

"I cannot help it if I was raised an aristocrat."

"You can be less of a pompous ass though."

He waggled his eyebrows, lifted her gloved hand and pressed a kiss to it. "I could, but you fell in love with this pompous ass, Duchess. I should hate to change now."

And then he strode off, in search of the card room. She watched him go, wondering if she and Gabriel would ever have such a comfortable rapport. With everything that was happening, they had not really got the chance to know one another. And that saddened her. She wondered how much of himself he had given away while he had courted her all the time pretending to be Cedric.

Her ruse worked, and it seemed that Cedric was unperturbed at not being allowed to dance with her. He simply shrugged and headed back to the card room. She did not see hide nor hair of him for the rest of the evening and that suited Kathleen fine. He was clearly still annoyed with her over the situation the other evening with the Duke of Kirkbourne. The Duke had also reported to her that Cedric was giving him a very wide berth this evening.

She arranged to leave the ball early so that she could meet Gabriel in the garden. Midnight was very early to be home. She popped into her Aunt Matilda's room to see if the old lady was still awake.

"Did you not enjoy the ball?" the older lady asked.

"Oh well, I turned my ankle slightly and could not dance. It is fine now but at the time it pained me. So I decided to come home."

"And was your betrothed there?"

"He was." Kathleen glanced around the room at her great-aunt's knick-knacks. She had so many things that had been brought over for this relatively short trip.

"Tell me, Kathleen, how do you really feel about the young man to whom you are betrothed?"

"Oh well, I barely know him. I have not had time to make any real judgements about him."

"You are being evasive, my dear."

"I am?" Of course, she was. Aunt Matilda may be old and cranky and occasionally a bit paranoid, but she was not an imbecile.

"You are. You marry him in but a few days. Have you even decided what you are going to wear?"

"Oh yes, I chose a dress when I went shopping with Lady Stal ... Lady Christina Marchby, oh, about two weeks ago. I should make sure I collect it. I had planned to take mama to see it, but I forgot. I am sure she will like it anyway. We can make a small posy of some of the evergreens that are being brought in to decorate the house."

"You do not seem overly keen to marry him. If you are not sure about it, Kathleen, you should speak to your father. He can find another investor."

Kathleen bit her lip and shook her head. "It is fine, Aunt Matilda. We just do not know each other properly yet." Oh, she hated lying to the old woman. She had to get out of this room. "Well, I am for bed. I am rather tired."

"You do look quite worn out. Are you sleeping?"

In truth, she was not sleeping particularly well, when she was not worrying about Gabriel, she was thinking about their times together and how he made her feel.

"Do not worry about me, Aunt. I am well. I think I am just fearful of missing you all when you return to America."

"But you shall have an exciting new life here."

"I know. I just love you all and shall miss you terribly."

"As we shall miss you, child. But we can still write, and we shall be over for Teresa's season in the summer."

Kathleen just hoped her family would speak to her after the scandal she would bring down upon their heads.

She nodded. "Well, I shall bid you goodnight." She glanced at the clock. She had half an hour to get ready for bed and sneak out into the garden. She was not ruining another ballgown. Her nightgown was much more practical, even if it was hardly appropriate. But she would have her pelisse over the top, and he was her husband.

∞ ∞ ∞

Half an hour later, Kathleen was in Gabriel's arms and Gabriel was kissing her as though both their lives depended on it. When she tugged on the button of his breeches, he placed his hand over hers.

"No, Kathleen," he said against her cheek. "Not again. You shall catch your death."

"I am fine. Please, Gabriel. What did you invite me out here for, if not for this?" She opened her pelisse and undid the buttons of her nightgown. She had worn this particular one because the buttons ran right down to her waist. She exposed one breast to him and lifted her hand to draw his head down towards it. He resisted for a second then his mouth was on it, licking, biting and sucking. She moaned as she ran her fingers through his hair, enjoying the sensations his suckling sent to her core.

"You are temptation incarnate woman," he said, raising his head and closing her nightgown. But when she managed to undo the fall of his breeches this time and stroked his already hard length, he allowed his head to drop back and surrendered to her touch.

Was it wrong that she enjoyed having this power over her husband?

"Please Gabriel, it is still days until we can be together. This may be our last chance. You just need to lift my nightgown and push inside me."

He opened his eyes and frowned at her. "Devil take it, Kathleen. I cannot resist you. Help me remove my coat." He offered her his sleeve and she helped him.

"Why?" When the coat was off, he placed it over her shoulders.

"I shall survive a little cold. I am used to it. You are not."

"I live in New Hampshire. It is much colder than this in winter."

"I care not. Keep that over your shoulders and lean on the bench. I swear to God, this is the last time."

She assumed the position she had the previous night and Gabriel removed his gloves, dropping them on the bench. He blew onto his hands and rubbed them together. When he lifted her nightgown and placed his hands on the cheeks of her bottom she smiled.

"Gabriel?"

"My hands are not too cold?"

"They are fine. They are warm."

He rubbed his hard length a few times through her folds, and she wriggled against his touch. The cold night air just heightened the sensations. Then he placed the blunt head at her opening, and she braced for him to enter her. But he waited for a moment, rubbing his finger over her pearl until she moaned and pushed back onto his shaft.

"Dash it, Kathleen. You are so eager."

He guided her along his shaft and set a rhythm. Then under her nightgown, he ran his hands up her body until he clasped his hands over her breasts. She had always been a little embarrassed by her large breasts and the way men would ogle them but, knowing that Gabriel liked them gave her a sense of empowerment. He kneaded the flesh with his hands then captured the nipples between his thumbs and forefingers, rubbing and pinching them and sending more pleasure to where they were joined.

Gabriel was pumping into her with abandon now and he slid one hand down to where they were joined to help bring about her release. When he lost his rhythm, he ground out an apology and withdrew from her. She turned in time to see him release onto the ground. He scuffed the seed into the ground with his shoes then fell to his knees in front of her. After his apology, Kathleen was a little perplexed. Why was he apologising and why was he now on his knees? His servant's clothing and this posture made her wholly uncomfortable.

"Hold on to the bench," he commanded. She did, and he lifted her nightgown enough that he could bury his head underneath. He pushed it up farther and then her leg was pulled over his shoulder. It was wholly ridiculous. But when his tongue lashed her wet folds and pleasure sliced through her, she did not care what tableau they created. Her only thought was to stop herself from crying out his name and alerting the whole of Mayfair to what was going on in the darkness of her parents' back garden. She writhed against his tongue and face and Gabriel pushed two fingers inside her, curling them and thrusting them frantically. She thought she may swoon with pleasure until suddenly the world shattered around her.

"Gabriel." The moan was torn from her as she tried not to make a sound. But he did not ease up. He continued to stroke with his tongue and pump his fingers in and out of her extending the release until she was completely mindless and the one leg she was supporting herself on started to give way.

Then Gabriel ducked out from under her nightgown, sucking his fingers and grinning. His wet chin glinted in the moonlight and his eyes sparkled with pleasure. He caught her up in a strong hold but kissed her gently.

"I apologise, My Lady. It was not well done of me to release first. But you will insist on being beautiful, passionate and altogether irresistible. A gentleman only has so much control."

"I did not mind. I quite enjoyed what you did after your release."

"Did you? I can do it again if you wish."

"I do, but you are correct, it is getting cold."

He frowned then. "Devil take it. I believe that Cedric has plans to go to a gaming hell and probably on to a brothel tomorrow night. He shall not be at the Hammond ball. I may just dress up and pretend to be him."

"He is going to a brothel?"

"Possibly." Kathleen was horrified. This was the man she was supposed to have married.

"Gabriel, that is awful."

"It is Cedric. Of course it is awful."

"But ... it is four days until we wed."

"You are not marrying him."

"But only a very few people know that. I must be a laughingstock."

"I suspect more people pity you than are laughing, my love. God alone knows what they will think when the truth is revealed."

"That my husband has little care that my betrothed may be going to a brothel." She really could not understand why he was being so flippant about it.

Gabriel wiped his hand over his face then drew her into his embrace. "I do care. I care so much I married you so that you would not have to lead that life. Let me be Cedric tomorrow night so that if the scandal and my sire's reaction is such that we are exiled from town for some time, then we will have had one last ball in London together. Please Kathleen, do not be vexed with me. I forget that you are still very innocent and not prepared to be exposed to Cedric's … less than appropriate habits. I have been aware of them for many years and do not flinch at them, no matter how distasteful. I apologise if you are distressed by them."

Kathleen sighed against his waistcoat. It was made of rough material. Nothing like the fine waistcoats he had worn when gadding about town with her. It was then she realised she still had his coat around her shoulders.

"You must be cold."

"Not really."

"I am not vexed with you. I am just … shocked, I suppose. Distressed that my father did not think to check that I was not marrying someone who had such distasteful proclivities."

"I doubt he is the only man in the *Ton* to spend his time in brothels. Though the brothels Cedric frequents do seem to be the less salubrious ones considering what he brings home."

"Brings home?"

Gabriel shook his head. "My love, you need not worry yourself. Please, think no more on it. I am your husband and believe me, I have no plans to stray. You are woman enough for me. You have quite enchanted me." He pressed a tender kiss to her lips. "Now go before you become ill with cold. I shall see you at the Hammond's ball tomorrow evening."

"Until then, my love."

She hurried through the garden, unwilling to look back. She had allowed him to remove the coat as she went and was fastening the buttons of her nightgown and pelisse as she reached the back door. Luckily the kitchen was silent. She hurried up the stairs and was nearing the top when Aunt Matilda appeared from the shadows— her face lit up by the single candle she held in her shaking hand.

"Oh. Aunt Matilda, you startled me."

"I would think I would when I have caught you sneaking into the house after a dalliance in the garden with a servant for the second night running. You and I need to talk, young lady."

Kathleen's blood ran cold, and she stepped down one stair as if she could run away from her aunt, but the concern creasing the old woman's brow brought Kathleen to a halt. Perhaps she could confide in Aunt Matilda.

Kathleen followed Aunt Matilda back to her room. Once back in the old lady's bedchamber, she was directed to a chair by the fire. She sat down and waited.

"I have watched you the last two evenings in the garden. I have a perfect view from my window. You were led in by a servant last evening and you went out to meet him this evening. I saw what he did to you. Did he coerce you?"

"No. Not at all."

"Then why? My dear child, why have you given your innocence away to a servant? He was the one you gave it to, is he not?"

"He is, but he is not a servant. Well, he is, but he is my husband, and he is an earl. Well, that is to say ... his title is an honorary one."

"An earl. But he is dressed as a servant."

"Yes. It is rather complicated."

"How can he be your husband if you are affianced to Mr Onslow?"

"I have no plans to marry Mr Onslow. He is cruel and visits brothels and is altogether unsuitable as a husband."

"He seemed quite pleasant on the few occasions I met him."

"That was not Mr Onslow. That was the Earl of Cindermaine."

"Pardon? The Earl of Cindermaine? Who is he?"

"The legitimate son of the Duke of Hartsmere."

"I am confused, child. I am an old woman. I sometimes cannot quite follow what is going on. It is my age. I fear old age does not come itself." Aunt Matilda tapped at her forehead in frustration.

"No Aunt. It is a confusing tale. This has nothing to do with your age. Gabriel, the Earl of Cindermaine and the heir to the Duke of Hartsmere, looks very much like his older half-brother Cedric Onslow."

"But he is in the country for he does not keep well."

"That is what the Duke wants everyone to believe. But he actually makes Gabriel work as a servant in his own household because of what the Duke thinks is a misdeed that Gabriel committed when he was but five years of age."

"And what was this crime?"

Heat burned up Kathleen's cheeks, but she was determined to soldier on. Gabriel had lived a terrible life and if he could overcome the odds, she could explain it to her great-aunt.

"I understand that the Countess—as she was at the time, Gabriel and Christina's mother, believed the affair between the then Earl and Cedric's mother to be over once Godfrey, the younger sibling was born. Gabriel, who was too young to understand about affairs and what happens between a man and woman, passed the dower house on the Marchby estate, saw his father spanking a woman as he had carnal relations with her. Apparently, his father is a brute and beat his wife and children. Gabriel was concerned for the woman and told his mama. The Countess, distraught at the news climbed to the ramparts of Marchby Castle and threw herself off. The Earl, who is now the Duke, has never forgiven the child who told tales and has punished him ever since."

"Good God, that sounds like some lurid gothic novel."

"I know."

"And so why did he end up gadding about town with you?"

"Cedric was ill. When he cast up his accounts, the first day he visited us, apparently he was quite ill and was abed for a fortnight. Gabriel, because he and Cedric both resemble the Duke, was made to impersonate Cedric. But he struggled to be quite as rude and obnoxious as his half-brother."

"But you do not know his half-brother. How do you know this is so?"

"I have heard enough people talk about him. His reputation precedes him. Besides, he is well again, and I met him a few nights ago at Lady

Arbuthnott's soiree. He was ready to drag me upstairs with him despite my protests and attempts to pull my arm out of his grip. And he would have, had it not been for the intervention of the Duke of Kirkbourne."

"Oh my!"

"I believe he is as much a beast as his sire, Aunt."

"Well. Now tell me, you said you have married this Earl of Cindermaine."

"We married three days ago. We would have left London by now but I wanted to have one final Christmas with you all and Gabriel has been so sweet about it. We plan to leave letters and leave on Christmas night. I know it is not well done of me to jilt Mr Onslow but I am sure he shall get over it and find comfort in a brothel, which is apparently where he shall be tomorrow night instead of the Hammond ball."

"I see."

"Anyway, it is done now and it cannot be annulled."

"Well, not from what I witnessed, it definitely cannot be annulled."

Kathleen closed her eyes and wished the floor would swallow her up. "I am sorry, Aunt. You should not have had to witness that."

"I could tell you were very much in love with the fellow. I did not watch for long. I just established what was going on."

"I still apologise. I believe I have more than a tendre for him. He only married me to stop me from having to marry Cedric but my feelings for him are stronger."

Aunt Matilda chuckled. "I have found, my dear, that men rarely do what duty demands and only do as they please. He has more than just duty on his mind. Even if he is only thinking with his manhood, then it is because he wants you permanently in his bed. He knows he shall deal well with you for a long time to come."

"He was worried that Cedric might beat me and bring home diseases from brothels to me. He is a good man, Aunt Matilda, and though we shall have no money, at least until he inherits his father's land, even then, his father need not leave his fortune to Gabriel, just the entailed estates."

Aunt Matilda pursed her lips and stroked her chin as she considered Kathleen's words. Kathleen was trying to think what else she could say in Gabriel's defence when Aunt Matilda held up her hand.

"Can you get a message to him to come here and meet me tomorrow morning?"

"I am sure that I could arrange it through his twin, Christina."

"You do that. Now go to bed and do not fret. Everything has a way of working out in the end."

Kathleen frowned at her aunt. She was taking this all too calmly. That would just make her worry all the more. Though she suspected that until this entire farce was over, she would not stop worrying.

Chapter 17

Christina burst into the kitchen the next morning, her face red and her eyes bright with concern and curiosity.

"Gabriel, Mrs Matilda Newham, the great-aunt of *Miss Kathleen and Miss Teresa Roberts*, is demanding that you visit her at home at eleven o'clock. She asks that you be dressed as a gentleman and that you attend her in the drawing room using your correct title."

"Do I have a title. My title is merely courtesy and my sire has never said whether I have the right to use it. We have all only ever assumed I am Cindermaine because that was how school addressed me."

"Then Cindermaine you are."

"I have no gilt-edged card to hand to the butler when I arrive."

"I had some made for you a couple of years ago. I always thought the day might come when you might need them. They are in my room. Come with me and I shall give you a book to return to Lord Stalwood for me."

"Another book?"

"I did not read this one. I just asked for one in case I needed to send you on an errand. I think ahead, brother dear."

"Ah, the wisdom of age, older sister."

"Shut up, Gabriel."

Gabriel chuckled and tugged one of her curls free from her coiffure.

"Oi, you beast."

"You adore me."

"I adore you so much I fought out of our mother's womb first to be rid of you."

"Ha. You were hoping they had changed the law and you could be Duke."

"Not if I'm anything like the current one, no."

"Well, feel free to stab me in the heart if I am anything like that brute."

"Worry not, brother. I intend to."

He grinned and followed her upstairs to her room. She produced some cards which already had his name and title neatly written on them. She also handed him a book.

"I thought you had read Mansfield Park."

"I have. My own copy is on that shelf. That is why I took Myles's copy. So that I would have no compunctions about giving it to you to return to him. I should hate to return a book I had started to read and was enjoying."

Gabriel chuckled. "You are a real bookworm."

"What else is there to do stuck in this mausoleum with Cedric and father."

"And Godfrey."

"Godfrey is fine when the other two are not around. I quite like him at times. He worships you. I think because, while you have been above stairs, you have been kind to him. Cedric is nasty to him and father ignores him."

"Poor Godfrey. I suspect he is not a bad fellow, but he is stuck with horrendous people for relatives and would really like to just be accepted by someone."

"Perhaps when this is all over, when Father is gone, we could accept him into our family as one of us."

"You mean, offer him what he never offered me?"

"Gabriel, you know it is difficult to stand up to Father."

"I did."

"You are a strong person. Godfrey did not have the education you did. He did not have the friends

266

you did—people like Myles and Lord Beattie. He had Father and Cedric browbeating him. Perhaps you got your strength from Mother."

"Mama was hardly strong, Chrissie. She killed herself."

"We cannot know what went on in that marriage, Gabe. They were married two years before we came along. One illegitimate child to his mistress either side of us being born. He beat us, so he must have beaten her."

"He did beat her. I saw him do it."

"So you can't know she was not strong. She may have been very strong and had to survive who knows how many beatings and injuries."

Gabriel ran his hand through his hair.

"Mayhap you are right. I judge her harshly because I ... well it matters not."

"You are still hurt by what you see as her defection. I know, Gabe. I still feel it too. She left us with that monster. And now our life is unfolding and it scares me. But we have survived thus far. We shall continue to survive. We have each other and Myles and Kathleen. And perhaps even Godfrey."

Gabriel chuckled. "Yes. Perhaps even Godfrey. I must get going or I shall miss the time for my summons."

"Do not be late."

∞ ∞ ∞

Gabriel made it to the front door of the Roberts' townhouse with only a couple of minutes to spare. The butler led him directly up to the drawing room, eyeing him suspiciously. Gabriel could not fault the fellow. He was wearing the same clothes he had worn while pretending to be Cedric and now he was claiming to be ... well ... himself.

He was shown into the drawing room and although it was not necessary because Kathleen's great-aunt was of a lower rank than he, Gabriel bowed anyway. He was used to bowing and scraping and frankly, it would do no harm to butter the old lady up—whatever it was she wanted with him. She pointed to a chair on the other side of the fire to where she sat and he accepted it.

"I shall get to the point. The last two evenings I have seen your assignations with my great-niece in the garden."

Gabriel raised an eyebrow. "I ... well ... that is to say ..."

"Save your excuses, young man. She has told me everything, My Lord. She has told me you are now my great-nephew by marriage and that you plan to run off with her on Christmas night."

"We have no choice, Ma'am. When word gets out, there shall be a great scandal and I cannot predict how the Duke will react."

"Where will you take her?"

"I plan to hide in plain sight. Therefore I shall not divulge that information."

"I see."

"And how will you support her?"

"I have friends willing to help me, but I plan to work. I have an education. We shall manage. For now, I must admit that my plans are not fully formed, Ma'am, since it was a rather hasty decision. Your great-niece was in danger were she to have married Cedric. My father beat my mother. I have reason to believe that in Cedric's case, the apple has not fallen far from the tree."

"And what about you? What assurances do I have that you will not beat Kathleen?"

"I love her. I would never harm her." Gabriel stopped after he said those words and drew in a deep breath. He had not even considered how he had really felt about the chit. He had called her *my love*. But that had just been an endearment. He had not supposed that he loved her. And yet the words had tripped off his tongue without thought as soon as he was grilled about how he felt for his wife. Did he love her?

"Good. She also loves you. You shall make a good match. Now as to your funds. Most of my money is in a bank in America. I need to find out how to have it sent to you. Kathleen is to get half of my wealth on my demise. She may as well get it now since you are both in need. Here." She waggled a sizeable coin bag at him.

"What is that?" he asked looking at it as if she were trying to hand him a live snake.

"It is gold coins. You can cash them in as you need to. Keep them on your person at all times from now on. Here is a belt my William always used to secrete his coins under his clothing. It is terribly old fashioned but it shall do the job."

"I cannot accept this, Mrs Newham. It is my job to support my own wife."

"You are supporting her by accepting help. Good God, boy, it sounds as if you have had no help and no family."

"I have my twin sister. She is all the family I need."

The old lady's face softened. "I'm sure she is, child, but a young girl has no say and no power to help you. You know that. Please let me help you. Society has let you down badly, and it is time for someone to step up. It is money I do not need, and it is money that Kathleen shall inherit anyway. Please take it now so that I know you are both safe. So that I know that *she* is safe."

Damn, she knew how to tug at his conscience. He sighed and held out his hand for the belt and the bag of coins.

"Thank you. I promise not to waste it."

"I have no doubt you are a frugal man after the way you have had to live. Do not be too frugal though. You deserve to live life. And my great-niece deserves happiness too."

"I promise to take great care of her."

"I know you will. Now, she is standing outside the door, desperate to know what is happening, would you be so kind as to open the door and invite her in and we shall have tea?"

He did, and Mrs Newham called out to the servant behind the door that they were ready for tea. When the door was closed again, Gabriel pressed a soft kiss on Kathleen's lips. Mrs Newham sighed and opened her fan and wafted it in front of her face.

They chatted about the Christmas entertainments and members of the *Ton* and about nothing in particular. The Roberts' house was now decorated for Christmas with evergreens over the mantel and a kissing bough near the door. He had never been allowed to be part of the festivities in his own house and had obviously never participated in visiting other people's homes over the Christmas Season, so this was quite a novelty for Gabriel.

When tea was finished Mrs Newham stood with her two canes.

"It is time for my nap. Now, Lord Cindermaine, I am sure you will find your way out in a timely manner. I appreciate you two are wed, but I would appreciate if you would not frighten the servants with your carnal activities in broad daylight. If you are determined to wait until Christmas Day to leave, you shall just have to keep your legs closed and your skirts down, Kathleen."

Kathleen groaned and hid her face in her hands as her great-aunt made for the door.

"Thank you, Mrs Newham."

"Thank you, My Lord, for saving my great-niece. I suppose you could make use of the Kissing Bough. As long as kissing is all you do. And do not get caught."

When the door closed Gabriel pulled Kathleen so that her still covered face was against his chest.

"My poor darling, are you terribly mortified?"

"Completely. She saw everything last evening and the evening before. My skirts up, you thrusting into me."

"You wanted to do it in the garden, my love. She does not seem too distressed. She did not pull smelling salts out of her bag once."

"You are making light of this."

"What would you have me do? What is done, is done. We can worry about something your great-aunt does not give a whit about or we can kiss under that kissing bough since tonight during our waltz, I shall have to dance with you the requisite distance apart so as not to start the tongues wagging of the gossip mongers among the *Ton.* Which shall it be?"

"I heard you say something about kissing. I heard nothing after that."

Gabriel laughed and stood, drawing her to her feet and walked to the kissing bough where he took her face in his hands and then pressed his lips to hers. Kathleen wrapped her arms around his neck and his arms moved around her waist and they kissed slowly, gently and passionately. When he started to harden in his breeches, he pulled away, lifted her hand to his lips and kissed it.

"Until tonight, my love."

"Gabriel?"

"Yes."

"Be careful."

He smiled at her. "You too."

Chapter 18

The Hammond's ball was a grand squeeze. It seemed as if everyone was in town for Christmas rather than on their country estates as they usually were. Perhaps the terrible weather over the summer had driven more people to seek solace in the town this winter. Things had not settled down yet.

Kathleen had arrived with her mother and her sister and she had soon sought out Christina to talk to.

"Gabriel is in the card room with Myles."

"They're betting?"

"Not proper money. There are a few high stakes tables but Gabriel and Myles are not stupid enough to gamble fortunes on games of chance. Credit them with some sense, Kathleen."

Godfrey came over at that point smiling at them. Kathleen was pleased to note he was wearing silk evening breeches and not inexpressibles.

"Ladies, I wondered if I might trouble you each for a dance."

"What about the third set? It's a set of country dances?" suggested Kathleen.

"That sounds fine. Thank you."

"You can put your name down on my card for the set after that then, brother dearest."

"Thank you, Christina. I am much obliged."

Christina smiled at him as he scrawled his name on her card. As he sauntered off the ladies moved closer together.

"He's not a bad old stick really, is he?" said Christina.

"No. Do you think he will tell anyone that Gabriel was here? He is bound to notice."

"I doubt it. When Cedric was not bullying Gabriel, he was bullying Godfrey. Perhaps we can find him a nice wallflower with a handsome dowry who does not mind that his family are all fit for Bedlam."

Kathleen chuckled. "That would be nice."

At that moment she felt a hand on the small of her back and looked up into sparkling brown eyes.

"What would be nice?"

"To dance with you," Kathleen said quickly.

"Since when did ladies ask gentlemen to dance?"

"It is an American tradition," she lied.

"Balderdash. However, it would be my pleasure to dance the waltz with you." He took her card and raised an eyebrow. "Mr G Onslow."

"He is harmless."

Gabriel smiled. "I am not disputing it." He wrote a C on her card next to the waltz.

"What does C stand for?"

"Well people will assume it stands for Cedric, but you shall know it stands for Cindermaine," he said in a low tone that only she could hear. "We need to talk, however. We are approaching Christmas rapidly and I wish to make sure we have a plan prepared for Christmas night."

"I agree."

"There is a small parlour on the first floor. The second room on the right. Meet me there after you have danced with Godfrey. It gives us half an hour before your dance with me."

"I shall."

Kathleen was enjoying the Hammond's ball. Christina was good company and when it came time to dance with Godfrey, he was solicitous and charming. He discussed topics which were banal but acceptable when the figures of the dance allowed them to converse. Kathleen liked it that way. Given the situation they were in, it was better to err on the side of caution.

When Godfrey returned her to Christina then bowed to his half-sister, Christina offered that they walk her back to her mother.

"I am fine. I shall go and find the ladies retiring room. I feel rather flushed."

"Are you sure? You should not be unaccompanied."

"I doubt I can come to any harm in the squeeze," she pointed out. Christina pursed her lips and looked unconvinced. "Go. The music is starting for the next set."

Kathleen turned her back on her friend and hurried out of the ballroom and towards the stairs and her rendezvous with Gabriel.

She arrived at the top of the stairs, slightly breathless and feeling terribly scandalous. Meeting a gentleman in a parlour at a ball. Indeed. Even though she knew he was her husband, no one else did. She opened the door of the parlour a crack to check that no couples were having a secret tryst in there. The last thing she wanted to do was interrupt young lovers having carnal relations on a love seat. But the room was quiet and apart from a fire burning in the grate, there was no light or sound. She slipped inside and stood next to the fire.

When the door opened a moment later, she smiled.

"I saw you slip in here, you naughty wench," he said in Cedric's voice as he moved towards her.

She laughed. "Please. Do not pretend when we are alone."

"Pretend what?" He had reached her and she could feel his breath on her neck. "God, I cannot wait to marry you on St Stephen's Day. Perhaps it would be wise to pre-empt our vows now, you saucy little minx. Is that not why you came in here. You saw me arrive at the ball and you wanted me to follow."

Kathleen's heart lurched and she suddenly felt light-headed. How on earth had she thought this was Gabriel? He did not even smell like Gabriel. His hands covered her breasts and squeezed. Not the gentle kneading she was used to from her husband but a rough bruising grab which she instinctively tried to wriggle out from.

"No Cedric. Please."

"Come, Kathy. We can get the pain of breaching your maidenhead out of the way now and then you shall enjoy your wedding night so much more. I know I shall because I can pump you so many more times."

Oh the very idea made her want to cast up her accounts.

"Cedric, let me go. I shall not marry you. Get your hands off me."

She was angry now, much more than she was frightened. How dare he manhandle her? She was still struggling in his hold when a shaft of light fell over them and a roar that sounded vaguely like Cedric's name was shouted.

"Let her go or I shall kill you."

It was Gabriel. He was here. And then Kathleen was stumbling backwards as Cedric let her go. She landed in a heap on her bottom, but she did not take time to assess if she was injured. She jumped to her feet to see Gabriel land a punch on Cedric's jaw. When Gabriel lifted his fist for the next blow, however, Cedric blocked it.

"I shall tell Father about this," whined Cedric.

"Tell who you damned well please," growled Gabriel. "Kathleen is my wife and we're leaving."

Well, that had certainly been one way to announce their nuptials, she supposed, especially when she looked at the door and saw a few people crowding around to see what the melee was about.

"Married? Since when?"

"Three days ago. The day Kirkbourne caught you trying to assault her at Lady Arbuthnott's."

"I was trying to take what is mine."

"She is *mine.*" Gabriel spat out the words individually.

"She is affianced to me. I shall have your marriage annulled."

"Not possible. She married me willingly."

"You are an imposter."

"She knows I am Gabriel Marchby, Earl of Cindermaine and that is what I signed on the marriage licence. I am no fool."

There were gasps from the doorway. It seemed that everyone must have assumed Gabriel was another of the Duke's bye blows. No one had even considered he might be the Duke's legitimate son.

"You are not leaving with her."

"Try to stop us, you snivelling little bastard."

Cedric's eyes widened at the word, and he threw a punch, but Gabriel was also quick and blocked it.

"Kathleen, head for the front door." He started to follow but Cedric grabbed his arm. Kathleen's mouth fell open when Gabriel lifted his foot and kicked him right in the groin. Cedric dropped to the ground with a high-pitched squeal of pain. But as he thudded on to the floor, he grabbed Gabriel's ankle. It seemed that Gabriel had perhaps even shocked himself at his own action and had taken a moment to react. Now Cedric had a death grip on Gabriel's foot.

Her husband kicked and pulled but to no avail. He at least managed to move Cedric's hands down as far as just having a grip on his evening slippers.

"Pull your foot out of your shoe," Kathleen whispered. Gabriel frowned, but he turned his ankle and eased his foot out of the slipper. And they were off, pushing and winding their way through the crowds of the ball. They were easily lost among the people, but Kathleen held tight to his hand. In fact, she wondered if the poor man would have any blood left in his fingers when they eventually made the front door.

"Shall I get your cloaks, Sir, Ma'am," said a footman as they rushed by.

"No, thank you," called out Kathleen as they pulled open the door and bounced down the steps of the Mayfair mansion.

"Come, we should head to Myles' house."

"No. You have been seen with him too often. Sarah offered us refuge at the Kirkbourne's. Their house is just a few minutes' walk away. But we should take the back alleys.

"Agreed."

They hurried down a side lane a couple of houses along from the Hammond's home and once out of the light of the streetlamps, Gabriel stopped her.

"Help me off with my coat."

"Why?"

"You need to put it on. You shall freeze to death in that thin ball gown."

"You shall freeze to death in that shirt, My Lord."

"Nonsense. Do you think I have warm blankets in my servants' quarters? Do not be ridiculous. I am used to the cold. You are not. Now for once in your life, Kathleen, obey my order."

Kathleen did not want to argue with him, and she knew he would be stubborn about this. She sighed and tugged at the sleeve of his coat. When it was off, he wrapped it around her shoulders.

"I fear we shall be in some mess by the time we reach the Kirkbourne house. We shall not be able to see the horse mess in the street and you have only one shoe."

"I am like Cinderella leaving a ball with only one shoe," he chuckled.

"I am sure Cinderella did not kick her step-sisters in the nether regions as she left, My Lord."

"Yes, that was instinct. I was so angry at him trying to take liberties with you."

"Never mind that now. Let us get to Sarah and Nathaniel's."

"Since when were you on first name terms with a Duke and Duchess," he teased.

"I am only on first name terms with Sarah, but it sounded silly calling him the Duke. Do you not think?"

"Perhaps."

They trudged down the alley groaning each time they stepped into a puddle or worse.

"My slippers shall be utterly ruined."

"I believe one of my stockings may just end up being buried in the garden to help the roses grow."

Kathleen giggled.

"I think we are nearly here. We need to go out onto the main street and check there is no-one around who would recognise us."

When they got to the main road, they peered around the corner. A couple were walking arm in arm towards them.

"Back," Gabriel hissed, then urged her into the shadows and up against a wall where he proceeded to kiss her thoroughly for a few minutes. He did not, however, press his hips against hers and whenever her hand started to roam down to his waist, he caught it and moved it back to his shoulders. Eventually, he pulled away and rested his forehead against hers. "If that couple walking by had seen us, I wanted them only to see a couple of young lovers engaged in a secret tryst. Not two people hiding from them and not a married couple copulating in an alley, much though I'd like nothing more than to lift your skirts and show you how I feel. Now, behave. You are about to enter the home of a duke and a duchess."

"Gabriel?"

"Yes."

"Before everything gets much worse—I mean in case we're caught and the Duke of Hartsmere causes problems, I just want to let you know that ..." She could not say it. Could she? "I think I might be falling in love with you."

He smiled and pressed a kiss to her forehead. "That is a shame. You have some catching up to do, Lady Cindermaine. I told your great-aunt today that I love you. Clearly, you were not listening hard enough at the door." And then he took her hand, checked the street and led her out before she could correct her earlier statement. She did love him. And now he thought she cared less about him than he did about her. Well, that was awful.

Would she get another chance before the evening was out? What a mess their lives were. She hated the Duke of Hartsmere. He was the cause of all their problems.

Chapter 19

Gabriel knocked on the door of the Duke and Duchess of Kirkbourne's town residence, hoping and praying that Kathleen had got the right of it and that the Duchess really had given them an open invitation to drop in unannounced in the event of an emergency such as this.

Of course, she was right about going to Stalwood's. Everyone knew that he had been seen all too frequently in the man's company over the past fortnight.

A butler opened the door, raising his eyebrows, no doubt because of the time. He looked like every other silver-haired English butler. His lips in a straight line, his eyes assessing and his nose firmly in the air.

"Can I help you ..." He left the lack of title hanging in the air.

"The Earl of Cindermaine to see the Duke of Kirkbourne," he said.

"Ah, come in, My Lord. My Lady." The man could not get out of the way fast enough to allow them to enter the house. "His Grace said if you arrived at his door, I was to grant you immediate entry whether he was home or not. He is home and in his study. I shall go and get him."

"No need Williams, I am here. Good God, man, you stink. Not you Williams, him."

"We had to come through the alleyways and mews to get here. I had to kick off my shoe to get Cedric off me. We're covered in horse muck. And the whole of the *Ton* now knows that Cindermaine is married to Cedric's fiancé."

Kirkbourne rubbed a hand over his face and scowled. "All right, I understand everything except the shoe. I think perhaps we should draw you both baths, get you cleaned up and then talk. We shall have the bath drawn up in the study. You can both go in there. It is warm We shall also prepare you a room. Or two? Which would you prefer?"

"One is fine." But he glanced at Kathleen. Perhaps she wanted two. Perhaps sleeping in the same bed with him was not something she had planned.

She nodded, smiling. She did not seem at all upset.

"Good, we shall get the bath organised."

"What is that smell?" They turned to see the Duchess wheeling herself towards them in a chair.

"Horse manure. They have just run the gauntlet from ... where?"

"The Hammond's ball."

"Really? So what happened?"

"Well, Gabriel asked to speak to me in a quiet parlour so that we could discuss our escape on Christmas night. It was dark, and I did not turn around when who I thought was Gabriel entered and unfortunately it was Cedric. And he put his hands all over me and I tried to break free, and he refused and then Gabriel came to my rescue. While they were arguing, Gabriel called Cedric a bastard and said he was Cindermaine. So I guess everyone now knows."

"I see."

"And then he kicked Cedric in the ... um ... well ..."

"Ballocks?" provided Gabriel. Kathleen rolled her eyes.

"Remind me why I married you? You are so uncouth."

"I ask Nate that all the time," Sarah said, laughing. "Now, come into the study and we shall organise the baths."

"I can do that, Your Grace," said the butler.

"Thank you, Williams."

"Now we need to send a servant around to the Stalwood residence to check on Christina and Stalwood. Let us hope they are aware of what is happening, and Christina has had the sense to go there and not Hartsmere House. I shall then send the servant to the Beattie's just in case they are followed from Stalwood's house."

"You're very good at subterfuge, Duchess," said Gabriel, grinning.

"We worked it all out the other night. Lord Beattie and Nate have been planning for this, just in case."

"And neither of you thought to mention it to me."

"You had enough to worry about. We had a feeling you would come to either of our houses and not Stalwood's."

"My first reaction was Stalwood's. Coming here was Kathleen's idea."

"Just as well you married a clever girl then since you are a dolt, eh, Cindermaine?" said the Duke.

Gabriel smiled ruefully. He would probably have reassessed the plan once they got out of the main street where the Hammond's house was. But his wife was possibly just a bit cleverer than he.

Once they were inside the study, Kirkbourne offered them the seats by the fire. Gabriel headed for one seat. When Kathleen started to move away from him to sit on the other seat, he caught her around the shoulders.

"No, come." When he sat, he placed her on his lap and cradled her against his chest. She was pale and starting to shiver and he was not going to let her go. Kirkbourne leaned against his desk and smiled indulgently.

"Would you like me to write to Stalwood?"

"Do you mind?"

"Not at all. You must look after your wife. She looks pale. I shall do it quickly and you can remain with her while she bathes. I will ask Sarah's maid and my valet to bring clothes for you both. My clothes should fit you. Sarah's gowns may be a little loose on Lady Cindermaine as they have extra give for her to use crutches.

"I doubt it. I have a huge bosom," Kathleen said.

Gabriel burst out laughing. "I am sure as a gentleman, His Grace has not been looking at your bosom."

Kirkbourne coughed and seemed to be scrabbling in his desk drawer for something. So, he had noticed her bosom. He supposed he could not blame the fellow. She had an amazing décolletage.

"I am sure marriage has not caused His Grace to go blind, My Lord," said Kathleen. "Rest assured, Gabriel, I can still see Cedric's manhood through his inexpressibles even though we are married. It is no less distasteful now than it was a fortnight ago."

"So you find it distasteful compared to mine?" Gabriel asked.

"Ahem." The Duke was glowering at them. "Do you two mind not discussing manhoods at this moment in time, especially not your bastard half-brother's, Cindermaine. Good God. I ate only a few hours ago. I should like it to remain in my body and not be cast up."

Gabriel grinned at Kirkbourne.

"As you wish, Your Grace."

"And stop *Your Gracing* me. Nate or Kirkbourne will suffice. That goes for you too Ma'am. May I be so bold to ask your permission to call you Kathleen since I know you are on given name terms with my wife?"

"Yes, of course, Your ... Nate."

He smiled at her then. "I shall write these notes and then I shall leave you to your baths. We shall be in the drawing room and shall have some tea and hot chocolate ready when you are finished. Something stronger if you prefer. Now I need to write some instructions for Stalwood. We need to make sure any messengers are not followed anywhere other than Beattie's."

"Are the Beattie's not in danger?" asked Kathleen.

"No, they are at Lady Rutherford's. Gideon's sister. I hate leaving Christina and Stalwood alone but Stalwood assured me he had some burly footmen who could handle the Duke's men. A few servants will set off to misdirect any followers. None will come directly here. Most will return to Stalwood's by a circuitous route. One will return via our back door. We are simply making sure that Christina is well and made it to Stalwood's from the ball."

Nate applied himself to the task and as the hip bath and a smaller basin and ewer were brought in along with steaming buckets of water, the Duke stood up.

"I shall leave you to it. Please do not worry. It will take around an hour for us to find out about Christina, but I am sure we will find her safe."

Gabriel nodded. He hoped Nate was right.

When the footmen were finished, a maid came in with some clothes and linens and introduced herself as Tilly, the Duchess's lady's maid. When Gabriel made no move to exit, she raised an eyebrow at him.

"My wife's safety is paramount, and I remain with her just in case anyone tries to get into Kirkbourne House. I hope you understand. I have seen her naked before."

"Yes, My Lord. I understand." She helped Kathleen out of her gown and Gabriel marvelled at the beauty of his wife. However, he scowled at the yellow bruises on her back. They were healing, of course, but they were extensive.

"Kathleen, Cedric brutalised you."

Kathleen shrugged. "I fell against the baluster. I fell hard, but it was … well, it was his fault, but it is over now. Please, Gabriel, there is no point upsetting yourself over it."

"I shall kill the bastard. It looks worse than it did the other day."

"Bruises always look worse a few days later."

She walked over to him and pressed a kiss to his lips. Devil take it. She was naked and kissing him in front of a maid. He scrunched his hands into fists and forced himself not to touch her.

"Calm down and sit. You are like a lion I read about in a book."

"You call me a cat."

"Cats are ferocious. And lions are the king of the jungle."

"I am a mere earl and just a courtesy one at that."

"You are a king among men to me, My Lord. Now, stop growling your disapproval and allow me to wash."

He moved away and sat down, as much to hide the bulge in his silk evening breeches as anything else. Soon she was washed and dressed, and Nate's valet had come in and helped him wash and dress as soon as the tub had been emptied and refilled. Gabriel felt bad that the poor servants were having to go to so much trouble so late at night. He knew how much work it was to heat water for baths and move the water and the tub and clean it. At least he and Kathleen hadn't brought home miniature friends from brothels, he mused.

"Are you ready?" he asked Kathleen

"Yes."

"We shall go and meet our hosts."

As they walked through the foyer, servants were cleaning the floor that they had dirtied when they arrived. Gabriel felt another pang of conscience.

"I am sorry," he said.

The maid just looked at him as if he had lost his mind. He supposed no one ever bothered to apologise for making work for her to do. It wasn't that Nate and Sarah were unkind, they had just been brought up to expect servants to earn their keep. The servants he worked with also would have given a visitor an odd look if they had apologised for dirtying the floor.

When they arrived in the drawing room, the Duchess and Duke were sitting side by side on a love seat. They looked relaxed and happy.

"Christina and Stalwood are fine. They are pleased to hear that you are here and will endeavour to visit in the morning when it will be easier to check if they are being followed. I have also received a note from Mrs Newham, your great-aunt, I believe, Kathleen."

"Yes."

"She said she has spoken to the family and while your father is upset about the business deal, she has explained the situation thoroughly and hopes that by the time he has slept on the matter, he shall be more amenable to your marriage. Hartsmere has already been there shouting the odds."

"That sounds like my sire. Look Kirkbourne, I appreciate the hospitality, but I worry about putting you, Sarah and your son in danger."

Nate waved him away.

"I have plenty of loyal servants and I've had weapons here ever since Sarah was shot just after we were married. It was only a flesh wound, but it frightened me, I can tell you."

"Who shot you?" asked Kathleen.

"Oh, that's a long story for another time. Suffice to say I survived and I am here to tell the tale, but we do not take our safety lightly. Nor that of our friends."

"You hardly know us."

"I hardly knew Nate when I married and fell in love with him. Friendship seldom needs time. When you know you like someone, you just know."

They drank their tea and hot chocolate in relative silence, all contemplating the events of the evening. Gabriel was half glad he'd been there to save Kathleen but wondered if she would have solved the problem on her own. She looked like she had been managing to get Cedric off her when he'd entered. However, Gabriel had seen red and his protective instincts had won out. He'd charged in without thinking of the consequences or checking to see if she could get herself out of the situation before revealing himself. It may have been a misstep. However, it was done now.

After tea, it was decided that they were all tired and ready for bed. Gabriel led Kathleen upstairs and assured Kirkbourne that they had no need of servants. He could see to his wife. Kirkbourne told him to ring the bell if they needed anything, and in the morning when they were ready to wash and get dressed. Nightclothes had apparently been laid out for them.

They bid him and Sarah goodnight and Gabriel led his wife into their bedchamber for their first night as man and wife.

∞ ∞ ∞

Kathleen could not understand why she felt nervous. Of course, this was their first night together, but they had consummated their marriage a few times. Somehow though, the idea of waking up with Gabriel in the morning seemed just as intimate.

He undid the ribbon fastening her gown and helped her out of it, then loosened her stays. She sat at the dressing table and undid the simple knot Tilly had fashioned for her earlier. Her hair was still damp in the braid it was still in. It had dried a little beside the fire while Gabriel had been bathing but it had not been nearly long enough.

Gabriel was out of his coat and waistcoat and had slipped off his shoes and stockings. He was standing behind her.

"May I undo your braid? I shall retie it before we go to sleep. I have not run my fingers through my wife's hair yet. I was itching to do it when you were bathing but did not want to upset Tilly."

Kathleen nodded and watched him as he ran his fingers through the long mane to loosen the braid. When at last his fingers moved freely, she moaned her pleasure and laid her head back against his stomach. He dropped his hands to her shoulders.

"You are exhausted. It has been a frightful evening. Come, the sooner we get to sleep, the better you shall feel."

"Yes." Was he not going to bed her tonight? Well, that was disappointing. He re-braided her hair but in a looser braid than Tilly had created and helped her on with her nightgown. He then removed the rest of his clothes. She noticed he ignored the nightshirt laid out for him and slipped into bed beside her.

He pulled her into his arms but she wriggled free.

"Why are you naked and I am not?"

"I never wear anything to bed."

"Well, now that we are wed, neither do I." And she sat up and pulled the nightgown off.

"Kathleen."

"Yes, My Lord?"

He ran a hand over her back and she grimaced. He was looking at those bruises again.

"Do they hurt?"

"No." She was telling the truth for the most part. They were slightly sore but nothing terrible. He shifted, and she felt the soft caress of his lips over her spine and then her ribs.

"I was not going to do this," he muttered. "I was going to let you rest."

"I do not need rest, Gabriel. I need you."

He continued to kiss her back as he snaked one hand around to cup her breast and pinch her nipple between his thumb and forefinger. She realised her hair was falling loose again. He had obviously undone his own braid and swiped the mane of damp blonde curls over her shoulder as he continued up her back and over her bare shoulder to her neck.

"How am I to resist you?"

He moved then, laying her gently back on the pillows then settling himself between her open legs. Then he just looked his fill smiling as he ran one hand up and down one of her thighs. He looked very pleased with himself.

"What are you thinking, My Lord?"

"That I am the luckiest man alive."

"Why?"

"Because you agreed to be my wife and you are perfect."

Kathleen looked down at her over-large breasts and grimaced. She suspected she also could do with losing a little weight around her hips and stomach too.

"I am not perfect, My Lord." Her gaze fell on the rippling muscles of her husband's stomach and the large thick shaft proudly pointing almost vertically and glistening at the tip. Now Gabriel was perfect.

Gabriel leaned over her and captured her mouth in a kiss. It was slow and sensual and did not contain the usual heat and desperation that his kisses had carried when they had been about to do the deed the past few times. His fingers caressed her body—her breasts, her stomach, her womanhood, her thighs, behind her knee. Tickles, caresses, pinches—all manner of sensations and Kathleen was aware of a slow burning desire in her, like a fire burning in a grate catching the coals. He moved over her, his shaft rubbing her most sensitive area but not penetrating her.

He broke the kiss and moved his mouth to her ear, biting the lobe gently.

"God, Kathleen, I need to be inside you soon." She ran her hands down his back. The skin was soft with a slight sheen of sweat already forming. Then she cupped his rounded backside and squeezed. He groaned and nipped her lobe harder before pressing his lips to her neck. He peppered gentle kisses down her neck along her collarbone and over her chest. When he moved and his hard length broke contact with the aching flesh between her thighs, she moaned her protest. He chuckled and pressed his fingers to her core to continue the delightful pressure. More pleasure spiked through her, and she rutted against his hand. His mouth covered one nipple and she gasped at the added sensations, moving her hand up to grip his hair and guide him.

"Gabriel, I want to give you pleasure too."

He lifted his head and grinned at her.

"Oh my love, I am experiencing much pleasure doing this."

"You are?"

He licked and suckled at her other nipple and made a sound as if he were eating a particularly delicious dessert. "I am," he breathed against the flesh of her ample breast.

Kathleen had not thought she could get more aroused when he had been on top of her and rubbing his shaft against her core, but it seemed that was untrue. When his fingers pushed inside her, she thought she may die of pleasure as his thumb strummed her pearl.

And then just when she thought she could take it no more, her body exploded in a burst of pleasure that burned through her from her centre to the tips of the toes and fingers to the roots of her hair. Little white lights sparkled behind her eyelids and Gabriel, who had seemed to realise it was about to happen and had moved up her body, smothered her cry of release with his kiss.

And before she had fully recovered, he was slipping his long, hard shaft into her, watching intently as he thrust, first slowly, then more quickly. She wrapped her legs and arms around him as he settled onto his forearms. His lips descended on hers and again her body started to burn with need. Her hips rocked in a counter motion to his. He broke the kiss.

"Dammit, you're so special, so passionate." His rhythm speeded up again and he held her gaze. She reached up with one hand and cupped his cheek. He turned his face to press a kiss to her palm, but he continued to thrust into her, and his gaze never left hers.

"I love you too, Gabriel." He grinned.

"I wondered how long it would take." Then he pushed a hand between them and teased her just above where they were joined. She writhed against him and knew another release was imminent. This time, when she arched her back and allowed the wave of pleasure to rush through her, she stifled her moan of pleasure. Gabriel cursed as his rhythm broke and he thrust a couple more time into her as his seed bathed her insides.

Gabriel collapsed atop her, and she pressed a kiss to his ear. When that did not make him respond, she swirled her tongue around the shell of his ear. He chuckled against her arm.

"What are you doing, wife?"

"I am finding out if you are alive."

"My heart is pounding out of my chest. If that constitutes alive, then I am well and truly alive."

He rolled off her and pulled her to him. "I should bank that fire. I forgot to do it before I climbed into bed. I am not used to a room with a fire."

"Are you not cold at night?"

"No. I am used to it."

"I see. I am always cold."

"Then you can have my share of the blankets. I just need one and a sheet."

"Even in winter?"

"Even then."

He climbed out of bed and banked the fire for the night then walked around to her side, urged her to sit up, ran a brush quickly through her hair and braided it. He washed between her legs before laying everything back on the dressing table. She loved how much care he took of her. It was very thoughtful. He then moved back around to his side, adjusted the covers so that she had most of them, blew out the single candle on his bedside table and closed his arms around her.

She ran her hand over his hips. She liked his hip for some reason.

He lifted her hand and pressed it to his lips.

"My darling Countess, I do hope you are not trying to commence round two. It is time for sleep."

"I was not. I was just ... enjoying the feel of you near me."

"Well, I suggest you enjoy the feel of me further away from parts of me that might think round two is commencing."

She chuckled and then drew a heavy sigh.

"What is the sigh for?"

"I am just aware how blessed I am. I do not believe I would be at all happy with Cedric. And yet by sheer chance, here I am with you. But it is not your title that means anything. If the roles were reversed, and you were the illegitimate son and Cedric the heir, I should still prefer you, because you are the better man."

He ran the tips of his fingers soothingly down her spine and back up before he spoke. "I am so very glad Stalwood, Beattie and Christina convinced me to marry you. Of course, I did not want you to marry Cedric but I must confess I did not think it possible to just take you to wife myself. And my pride was hurt at the idea of accepting money from friends to support us."

"I think father shall come around and give us my dowry."

"Did your great-aunt not tell you?"

"Tell me what?"

"She is giving me your inheritance from her. She has already given me a bag of coins. That was in the belt I had around my waist. It is sitting over there."

"I ... I saw no belt. I ... was looking at your bottom when you were getting undressed."

He snickered like a horse and patted her bottom. "I like your bottom too."

"Tell me about the inheritance and stop talking about bottoms, Gabriel."

"You started it. When she called me to your home this morning she gave me gold coins which I can take to the bank and trade for money. She said she shall send the rest when she gets back to America."

"I see."

"And this is my inheritance, from her."

"Apparently so. You are to get it when she dies. I tried to say no, but she made me feel terribly guilty and that I would be allowing you to starve if I did not take it."

"She is good at manipulating people. Do not feel bad. So we have some money to start out with."

"It appears so. I shall invest it. Stalwood is good at investing. I believe so are Beattie and Kirkbourne. I shall take their advice."

"Good."

"You sound sleepy, my love."

Kathleen curled onto her side with her head on his shoulder.

"I am. I should have liked to have made love again like we did on the day of our wedding but

...” she yawned suddenly and stretched her limbs to try to make herself more comfortable in the strange bed. Gabriel kissed the top of her head.

"We have years ahead of us." He tilted her chin and kissed her lightly. "Until tomorrow. Good night, my love." Then he threw most of the blankets over her and settled her against his side.

Chapter 20

Kathleen woke and peeked through the curtains of the bed, aware that it was daylight. So it must be quite late. She glanced at Gabriel and was unable to stifle the laugh that escaped her. The fire had obviously been set sometime in the early morning and Gabriel must have found it too hot because he had turned onto his stomach and had just a corner of the sheet covering his back. His bare backside and his legs stuck out from the small portion of the sheet. She had a terrible urge to sink her teeth into that perfect round curve.

Her laugh must have woken him because he lifted his head with a start and peered around through half-closed eyes. He blinked a number of times and Kathleen was sure he was trying to work out where he was and what exactly was going on. He glanced at her and his lips slowly curved into a smile as memories of yesterday must have started to come back to him.

"Kathleen?"

"Yes, Gabriel."

"What time is it?"

She glanced at the clock on the mantel.

"Just after nine o'clock."

"Good God, I have not slept until this time since I was at Oxford."

He turned over and pulled himself into a sitting position. It was then that she noticed he was already hard. He followed her gaze and grimaced.

"Gentlemen sometimes wake up already hard. We call it a morning cock stand." He shrugged.

She moved towards him and pressed a kiss to his lips allowing the sheet she had been holding against her breasts to fall. Gabriel deepened the kiss and then urged her to straddle his legs. Soon their tongues were stroking each other's hard and fast and Gabriel's fingers were caressing her body everywhere. She moaned into his mouth as she slid her wet heat against his hard shaft.

"Gabriel, this feels lovely," she whispered against his mouth.

"It is supposed to," he chuckled.

"First thing in the morning?"

"There are no rules as to when a man and his wife can make love. Now lift yourself up." She did and he clasped himself and positioned the tip of his erection at her opening. She cast a doubtful look at him, but he nodded encouragingly.

"Sit back down, slowly and carefully."

"Are you sure, Gabriel?"

"I am, but if, once you try it, you dislike it, we can roll over and do it the way we did last night."

She slid down his shaft and once fully seated atop him she let out her breath slowly.

"This is how we men ride horses," he said, a smile curving his lips.

"Are you calling yourself a horse, My Lord?"

"I am yours to command, My Lady, just like a horse."

"It feels rather odd. You feel bigger."

"I'm just deeper inside you. Is it hurting?"

"No." "

"Then try moving." She did and soon she was moving with abandon until they were both crying out their releases.

Kathleen thought afterwards that perhaps she could get used to having marital relations in the morning because the rest of the day, despite the difficulties and the travel, went by in a haze of happiness because she only had to think of Gabriel's face as he spilled his seed into her and she felt all warm and tingly.

Kathleen supposed married life to the Earl of Cindermaine may very well suit her.

∞ ∞ ∞

"What is the matter, Gabriel?"

"Nothing. It is snowing." Gabriel was staring out of the carriage window, worry gnawing at him. They must be ten miles from Marchby, and the sky was dark and heavy looking. Large flakes of snow clouded his view, so it was probably on for the duration. Kathleen leaned past him to look out.

"It is so pretty."

"It is not pretty, Kathleen. It is damned dangerous for the horses. What if we get stuck in it?"

Kathleen snorted. "Gabriel, the horses will be fine if we slow down. It is not icy underfoot, so they will be making the trail and if the carriage gets stuck, then we dig it out. I have lived in New Hampshire and Boston all my life. This is nothing. We have this amount of snow in November. We can be waist deep in it on occasion. Really, there is no need to be such a ... such a ..." She waved her hand dismissively.

He sat back in his seat and scowled at her.

"English drivers and horses are not used to the snow. It is different here."

"We shall cope. Stop looking so worried. We have overcome so much already. Even my father is coming around."

"He threatened to cut my ballocks off, my love."

"Only at first. Then Nate described what happened at Lady Arbuthnott's house and I explained what happened at the Hammond's and he calmed down considerably. Mama said she will talk to him. She can be quite formidable."

"Hmm, it is a pity she has not passed that trait onto her daughter," Gabriel mused, the sarcasm dripping from his tone.

"I am only formidable when you are vexing me, My Lord."

They rode on for miles and every time that Gabriel looked out the window and frowned, Kathleen clucked her tongue and shook her head as if he was being a fussing old lady. Each time he sat back, she patted his arm soothingly. He had called out of the window a couple of times to ask the driver if he was well, and the driver had assured him that a little snow never killed anyone. Gabriel suspected that was not, in fact, true but chose not to comment for fear of being berated by his wife.

Eventually, the carriage rolled into the Marchby estate. Kathleen craned her head to see out of the window and marvelled at the fourteenth-century castle which had been fully maintained and updated as the years had gone by.

Gabriel's gaze shifted to the tower and the battlement where his mother had jumped to her death and coldness crept into his bones. Had this been a bad idea?

"We have a bright future ahead of us Gabriel. The past cannot be undone, and no one can remove your memories, but we can make happy ones here."

It was as if she could read his very thoughts.

"I have no idea what you are talking about, My Lady" he answered stiffly. Kathleen's jaw tightened, and she nodded and turned to look back out of the window, but the hurt in her eyes was unmistakable.

He wrapped his arms around her and kissed her neck, his hand slipping up to cup her breast.

"I love you," he said.

She shrugged out of his hold and he pushed himself back against the squabs. She may as well have slapped him on the cheek.

"You are angry with me," he said.

She sighed. "Not angry. Disappointed. First, you snap at me for trying to be understanding and helping you see a brighter future, then you think that kissing me and massaging my breast somehow makes your outburst better."

"Devil take it, Kathleen. I am doing the very best I can. I am not used to …"

"You have already used that excuse, Gabriel. I am not society. I care not if you spill your tea in your saucer then do not know what the protocol is. I care that you apologise when you are in the wrong."

"Was I in the wrong, or were you patronising me, My Lady?"

"It was not patronising. Gabriel, we shall survive, and we shall be happy—if not here, then somewhere. If not with servants and carriages and balls during the Season, then with each other in a cottage in the country. We shall have each other and our children. We have Christina and Myles, Aunt Matilda, Lord and Lady Beattie, the Duke and Duchess, and hopefully my parents and Teresa. But if not, we shall still manage. We have each other and I am sure I can find someone who can teach me how to do household chores. You are not afraid of hard work."

"But you looked so excited when you saw the castle."

"It is lovely. But if it is not to be ours, then so be it. But please, tomorrow is Christmas Day. Let us enjoy Christmas and everything that goes with it."

The carriage came to a halt and the butler came out to see who it was. Gabriel descended the steps and handed his wife down. He looked at Foster, the butler who had been with the family since … well, forever. The butler's normally straight facial expression turned to a frown as he tried to work out which brother he was dealing with. Gabriel smiled and the old man's face relaxed.

"My Lord?"

"Foster. It is good to see you."

"Your father has relented?"

Gabriel grimaced. "No. I rebelled, I suppose. It is a long story, but I have no idea how he shall react once the story comes out, so we came to the country to see how it all plays out and to escape his wrath. May I introduce Lady Cindermaine? We married a few days ago."

"Many congratulations, My Lord, My Lady."

"I know it is a terrible inconvenience but will cook be preparing dinner tonight. We can try to go to the inn in the village."

"Of course it is no inconvenience, My Lord. It is hours until dinner. We shall have the best dinner prepared for you."

"I hate to be a burden."

"My Lord, we are here to serve you. It is what we are paid for. Please think no more on it."

"But I am one of you, Foster."

"No, My Lord. We may have accepted you as one of us because it was a necessity, but it never sat comfortably with us. You can have no understanding of the relief I feel to have you in your rightful place. An earl should not be cleaning boots and sewing shirts, especially not those of his illegitimate half-brother. But here, I am keeping you outside talking in the snow. Let me get you inside and I shall have a tea tray brought to you in the drawing room while we have your rooms prepared."

He brought them into the large imposing hallway with a grand staircase sweeping up to three or four storeys above. The high ceiling with the huge candelabra filled with unlit candles was imposing, but the room was well lit with candles in wall sconces. It had initially been the great hall of the keep before the castle had been extended.

"Tea would be wonderful, Foster," said Kathleen. "I am quite frozen to the bone."

"I shall show Lady Cindermaine to the drawing room. Is the fire on?"

"Yes we light it every day, just in case. Um, My Lord, which bedroom would you like to use? The previous earl, your father ..."

"My sire, yes ..."

"He did not use the chamber meant for the Earl. He used the bedchamber that was prepared by a previous Earl for a visit from the King. I am not sure which King it was, but that is why the bedchamber is so grand. He was the first earl to use that particular set of suites.

"Which room did his countess use?"

"She used a minor bedchamber that was near the nursery, My Lord. She liked to be close to you and Lady Christina."

"So, she did care for us after all, at least a little."

"My Lord, your mother loved you, begging your pardon for being so bold. Your father, begging your pardon again, but suffice to say that the woman did not have her troubles to seek and none of us servants was terribly surprised that her life ended as it did."

"Tell me, Foster. I am a child no more."

Foster glanced warily at Kathleen then decided to obey a direct command.

"He beat her."

"I know. He beat me too."

"We would bandage her up and set her broken limbs as best we could, My Lord. He would also force himself upon her, sometimes in public areas of the castle. One time your nursemaid was only just ahead of you and Christina and rounded a corner and had to turn quickly and shuffle you away lest you saw what he was doing."

"Yet he does not beat his mistress and bastards."

"I would not be so sure about that, My Lord. Cedric and Godfrey had some interesting injuries over the years, and they did not get them falling out of trees. Your mother was very unhappy. Why she chose that day to throw herself from the battlements no one will ever know. She did not leave a note. You told your father what you did. You were sobbing and telling him it was your fault. You were just a babe and unable to hold your tongue."

Gabriel frowned. Had he? He did not remember. Or did he? A memory of hiding under his father's desk crying. His father accidentally kicking him as he sat down and Gabriel confessing what he had seen and what he had done.

"Oh God. I blamed her all this time."

"Which way is the drawing room, Foster?" he heard Kathleen ask, but his mind was a jumble of long-ago memories. His father beating him to within an inch of his life. His father stripping him naked and leaving him on the battlement off which his mother had thrown herself for two days. It had been the middle of December. His father making him clean every piece of brass in the castle until it shone.

Gabriel was sitting by the fire, Kathleen kneeling at his feet, his hands in hers as she kissed his knuckles and looked worriedly at him.

"What?" he asked. "Why are you looking at me like that?"

"You have been in a daze for nearly a half hour. The tea shall get cold soon."

"I …"

"I know. Gabriel, you do not need to talk about it if you do not wish to, but I am here to discuss it if you would like to."

He nodded. "I remember a lot and it is very vivid. So many memories I have buried. Perhaps they were too painful. He was a worse brute than I can remember."

"It would appear so. Your poor mama."

"Thank you."

"For what?"

"It seems that I have become fit only for Bedlam and you have, like the true lady that you are, stepped in and taken charge."

She chuckled. "I may be American, but they do teach us how to be ladies."

He drew her up and onto his lap. "Not too much of a lady, I hope."

"Gabriel, not in the drawing room."

He grimaced. "Hmm, no. I would hate to be like my sire."

"You are nothing like your sire. It sounds as though he took your mother by force. I do not need to be forced into your arms. However, we do not wish another situation like Aunt Matilda spotting us in the garden."

"God no." But he kissed her anyway. When he withdrew, she lifted his hand and kissed it on the back.

"Come, will you show me around your castle?"

"Of course."

They spent a happy hour with Gabriel showing her where they would be sleeping, the portrait gallery, the living areas, the parts of the castle that were just for show, the large ballroom and the nursery. They were walking along the corridor from the nursery when Kathleen stopped.

"Where does that stairway lead?" Gabriel shuddered inwardly, but he drew in a breath.

"The battlements."

"Can I see?"

Could he show her where his mother threw herself to her death and where his father had locked him outside in the freezing cold for two days?

"It is snowing."

"Just because you refuse to go up there Gabriel, does not mean it is not still there."

He turned a narrow gaze on her. "What the devil do you know about it?"

She bit her lip for a moment but then her chin lifted, and she laid a hand on his chest. "You are a grown man. You have faced down so many demons these past few days and you have faced down your father."

"I ran from my father like a coward. I have not faced him."

"You faced him when you were younger—when it was necessary—to stand up for your sister. Do you not think in these last couple of days, Christina has not told me of your life since? She spoke frankly in the carriage to Richmond, Gabriel. Your sister is no shrinking violet. I know more than you think."

He grabbed her hand and marched up the staircase, turning the key that was already in the lock and pulling her unceremoniously out into the snowy twilight.

"Is this what you want, Kathleen. For me to bare my soul to you?" Anger, fear, rage, hurt, pain, grief, confusion roiled within him as he turned in the snow in front of her. "Do you want to know where she jumped to her death? Because I do not know which part of the battlement she jumped from. I did not see her crumpled body. My nurse protected me from that pleasant view, Kathleen. Now what? Do I weep? Do I forgive my mother? Do I forgive my father? Good God, I have not called him father in years. You are bringing out the sentimentalist in me. Perhaps you just wanted to see the pretty view and the snow. Come to the wall and look your fill, my love."

He urged her over, knowing full well her slippers would be ruined by the snow. But she came anyway.

"Are you finished?" she asked when she stood on the ramparts and looked over the edge.

"Not nearly. I still do not understand your motivations for wanting me here. Did you want to see how far a drop it was? Do you fancy it would be nice to see how far my mother dropped to her death? Or do you want to see where I was left for two days, as a five-year-old, naked and scared and freezing while my father got the start of his revenge on me for my bad behaviour."

"Oh Gabriel," Kathleen said, swiping at her tears then drying her hands on her gown before reaching up and wiping at the tears on his cheeks. He had not realised he had become a pitiful emotional wreck.

Kathleen wrapped her arms around him and he, in turn, wrapped his arms around her and buried his face in her neck. He did not know how long they stood there but when a weak shiver ran through her, he realised she was standing in the snow in a thin gown. He, at least, had a woollen coat.

"I apologise. That was cruel and unnecessarily unkind."

"It was honest. I want you to always be honest with me, Gabriel."

"I should not have brought you out here."

"Yes, you should have. Coming out here and letting out all the hurt and anger that has been pent up for twenty years can only help to heal you, Gabriel."

"Healing is over-rated."

"Not if you become whole and are able to become a better father and husband than your own father as a result."

"I would never be like him."

"I know but you must learn to accept what happened as being in the past."

"You make it sound so easy."

"It shall not be easy, but I shall be with you as you deal with it."

"Is this why they made you vow to remain with me for better or worse?"

"I believe it is. But you shall always be the better man, Lord Cindermaine."

They walked back inside, arm-in-arm, and the rest of the evening passed quietly. The staff were all delighted to see Gabriel in his rightful place again and a maid was appointed to look after Kathleen until arrangements could be made for Patsy to be brought to Marchby Castle, assuming the maid wanted to come to the country.

They made love long into the night and fell asleep in each other's arms, contented and looking forward to Christmas morning.

Chapter 21

Christmas day was unlike anything that Kathleen could ever have imagined. Gabriel refused to have dinner served in the dining room since they had turned up unannounced on Christmas eve with no warning to the staff. Instead, they had a quiet morning walking to church, the church service, then a large Christmas lunch in the staff quarters with all the staff in attendance. Gabriel had threatened them all with dismissal if anyone was anything less than jolly because he and his wife were in attendance.

At first, the atmosphere was rather stilted, and Kathleen feared that they were ruining everyone's Christmas until Gabriel started to reminisce about some of the things he had got up to as a lad. Usually in his role as one of the servants—such as when he had placed manure inside Cedric's boot or when he stitched closed the cuff of his father's favourite coat.

Everyone began to relax then and told their own tales of life below stairs. It was fascinating. When it came to Kathleen, she was able to tell them of the long voyage from America and what it was like to be on board a ship for six weeks. All about her poor sister casting up her accounts for days and about the handsome sailor who tried to get her to marry him. Gabriel did scowl at that part of the story. And everyone chuckled when she pointed this out.

They spent the evening in the drawing room drinking tea, playing cards and reading—just the two of them together and Kathleen thought she could be quite content if this was her life. Gabriel was excellent company.

Once again, when they went to bed, he took her to the heights of pleasure and afterwards she fell asleep, sated and content in his arms.

By afternoon on St Stephen's Day, Kathleen was feeling the most content and happy she could ever remember feeling. They were wandering through the snow near the dower house when she spotted a carriage with outriders trundling up the private road to the castle.

"Gabriel, who do you suppose that is?"

He narrowed his gaze and squinted at the carriage.

"That is the ducal coach. It appears Hartsmere has found us and wants his pound of flesh. Come."

But instead of leading her to the castle, he led her to the dower house. He opened the door and led her in. The place smelled musty and unlived in. It was cold and damp and Kathleen shivered involuntarily.

"What are we doing?"

"Let him wait," said Gabriel turning his wife into his arms and popping the buttons on her pelisse.

"Gabriel, do you mean to tumble me here?"

"Do you have a problem with your husband making love to you?" He had enough buttons on her pelisse undone now that he had access to her neck and started pressing kisses to it.

"I do when you are tumbling me just to get some sort of strange revenge on your father. Are you hoping he shall come looking for you and see you taking me from behind and slapping my arse?"

Gabriel stilled at that. She was not sure if it was her use of the word "arse" or the idea she had put in his head. But he frowned.

"I apologise."

"I am not some courtesan you can use to get revenge on your father. I am your helpmeet. Do not treat me like a possession, Gabriel."

"I have hurt you, have I not?"

"No. But if we make love now, then we make love. We do not have sex to seek revenge on your father. If, in the process, he has to wait for us to return to the castle and it inconveniences the Duke, then that would be a terrible shame. Would it not?"

"It would be," he said mockingly.

"It would seem a little rude."

"I agree."

"Almost as if we do not respect such a refined gentleman of the *Ton.*"

"You mean, almost as if I thought he was a blaggard who is not worthy of my time?"

"Indeed."

"That would be terrible."

"It would," she said, pulling his head down towards hers and undoing a couple of buttons at the front of her gown so that she could free her breast to his touch. Thank goodness she had foregone stays this morning.

He kissed her as though he was a starving animal, and her lips and mouth were his last meal. The tension in his muscles told of a man out for revenge but scared to let go in case he hurt her.

"I cannot, Kathleen. This is revenge. Not love."

"Then love me. Like you did at the inn, in the garden, in the boating shed, in our bed. Forget about what happens when we leave here. The only revenge we are truly seeking is keeping a self-important man waiting. The rest should be about our pleasure." She leaned over the couch and started to pull her skirts up.

"What are you doing?"

"I thought you would want to do it this way because ..."

"No, this is about our pleasure. I did it that way in the garden because there was little choice. Come, let me lay you on the chaise and make love to you properly.

And he did. He took a long time laving and sucking at the most sensitive parts of her body. When eventually he undid his breeches and sank into her, she had released three times and was mindless with the need to feel him inside of her.

He moved slowly at first, kissing her neck, collarbone, ears, face and lips. He was increasing the need in her own body. When she urged him to go faster by digging her booted heels into his backside, he growled into her neck.

"You drive me to Bedlam, My Lady."

"I believe you have taken me there three times already, My Lord."

He chuckled, gathering her closer as he increased the speed of his thrusts.

She screamed her release moments before he pushed into her hard and stiffened. His features grimacing and the warmth of his seed filling her.

"God, I love you so much," he managed as he rocked slowly in and out of her, his breathing laboured as he finished spending himself completely.

"I shall always love you. No matter what happens when we go back to the castle, remember that you are mine and he can take away financial support and the roof over our heads, but he cannot take away our love. And we have Aunt Matilda's money."

"Indeed. We have that."

"And we have friends, Gabriel. Good friends."

"We do."

"If the worst comes to the worst, we take Kirkbourne's carriage and head for his estate. That's where he said to go." He did not seem pleased with the idea. Kathleen sighed. Tears sprang to her eyes unbidden, and he scowled.

"What is the matter?"

"It seems that our love is enough for me but not enough for you. Which is odd since you were the one who grew up with nought and I was pampered and spoiled. How things have changed."

"You are enough for me. But you deserve more than this."

"I want *you*, Gabriel. Only you. The rest is like icing on a cake. Pretty and tasty but it is too much eventually, and it is not filling and wholesome. Love and family are what is filling and wholesome. I could have had the icing with Cedric and I would have been miserable and probably bruised and ... well, not given a choice if I did not want to bed him."

"But you would have had money."

"And what if one day he hit me, forcing me somewhere I did not want to go, like the night at Lady Arbuthnott's then let go and I hit my head and died, My Lord? It happens. Look at Patsy's husband. There are no pockets in shrouds."

He raised his eyebrows and pursed his lips.

"You make a good point, My Lady."

"We have kept the Duke of Hartsmere waiting long enough."

She batted at him until he moved off her and adjusted her clothing as best she could. Gabriel fixed his own clothing before helping her with the lacings of her gown.

∞ ∞ ∞

They put back on their outdoor clothing and returned to the castle. The ducal coach with its ostentatious emblem still stood outside the front door. A couple of footmen, whom Gabriel recognised, stopped when he approached the door. He smiled at them and was surprised when they bowed. These were men with whom he had supped ale in an inn.

He led Kathleen under the large portico of the castle and through the front door which was held open by the butler.

"I see he is here. Is he in the drawing room?"

"Yes but, you..."

"Fine. Don't bother to send up tea. He is not staying."

"But ..."

Gabriel sent a wave over his shoulder that suggested he cared not what the butler had to say. When he got to the drawing room doors there were two servants standing guard like sentries or footman. Why the devil did he have footmen at his drawing room all of a sudden? He supposed it was because a duke was here.

"Kathleen, my love. My father and I have a fraught relationship. Please ignore anything he says or anything I say. Just know that I love you and anything I say is to wound or shock him, not you."

She nodded stoically.

He nodded to the footmen who looked a little concerned and strode in as they opened the door.

He began speaking before he even looked towards his father.

"Sorry, Your Grace, I was tumbling my countess in the dower house. You know what a draw that place has."

He stopped as Kathleen nudged his side and hissed his name. His gaze settled on Godfrey who had jumped to his feet and was standing wringing his hands.

"Where's ..." Gabriel started, but he stopped when Godfrey executed a low bow.

"Good afternoon, Your Grace."

Gabriel's gaze did a quick search of the room, but his father was certainly not here. He looked behind, but the man had not appeared in the doorway after him.

"If you are calling me Your Grace, Godfrey then ..."

"Our sire is dead, yes. You are the ninth Duke of Hartsmere. I am your humble servant." He bowed again.

"Up Godfrey. Please stop grovelling. Tell me, he is dead?"

"Yes, Your Grace." Godfrey sighed. "Well, you can imagine he was in a real temper about your defection and marriage. He went to see ..." he gestured to Kathleen. "Uh, Her Grace's father and was not pleased with the result of the meeting. Apparently, her father is considering giving her dowry to you and funds to set you up. Not that you shall need them now." Godfrey shook his head, clearly getting himself back on track. "But he came out of the Roberts' townhouse in a foul temper. Cedric called out a warning as he crossed the road, but Father was so busy railing and shouting back at Mr Roberts and threatening him with ruin that he did not hear, or he ignored Cedric's warning and a coach and six, which apparently was going at some speed for a town street, ran him down. The horses trampled him and there was nothing could be done to save him."

"I may ask one of those young men outside the door to arrange a tea tray after all," said Kathleen as she led Gabriel to a love seat and urged him onto it before patting his knee. He clasped her hand briefly then let it go. He felt like he had been trampled by horses himself. He despised his father, but he'd not prepared himself for this.

"And Cedric?"

"Shocked but fine."

"You came in the ducal carriage."

"I thought you would want to ride home in it. Did I overstep the mark? I am sorry, Gab ... Your Grace."

Gabriel waved a dismissive hand at him. "You are still my half-brother. Gabriel is fine."

"Tea is on its way."

"About the coach, old boy, I was only doing what I thought was right."

"It is fine, Godfrey. It seems sensible to bring the ducal coach if I am, after all, the Duke. Good God." He shuddered visibly. He had known this day would come but the idea of it was quite sobering. And he had been prepared for a showdown with his sire. The feeling of anti-climax was quite, quite overwhelming. He stood—unable to sit still and paced to the window. "When did it happen?"

"Yesterday morn. The Duke decided he was going to spoil the Roberts' Christmas morn. I suppose that was why the coach was travelling so fast. He did not expect anyone to be out at that time on Christmas morn except a few servants and they would be looking where they were going."

"How are Cedric and your mother taking the news?"

"Cedric is in shock. He said the Duke's body was badly broken. He does not have a strong stomach, as you know. Mother is being stoic. She seems ... relieved. She was even asking if she had to go into mourning since she was his mistress."

Gabriel raised his eyebrows. "I suppose there are no rules for mistresses. We shall have to purchase mourning clothes as soon as we get back to town. How will we tell Christina?"

"I sent a messenger with a note for Stalwood to his Richmond estate. I assume they would have gone there because of the weather."

"Yes, they did. Godfrey, why are you doing all this?"

"All what?"

"You came here, you have arranged for Christina to find out. What else have you organised?"

"Just for Father's solicitor to attend you once you return. Gabriel, I did not mean to overstep the mark. I merely ..."

"You have not. I just want to know why you, the youngest of my siblings has had to take charge."

Godfrey blink then pursed his lips. "Cedric is an arse."

Gabriel felt the bubble of laughter explode in his throat before he roared with glee and lurched forward to slap his half-brother on the shoulder.

"Indeed he is, brother. Indeed he is."

Godfrey looked rather nonplussed, and Kathleen just looked amused as the tea tray was brought in.

"You must be hungry Godfrey."

"I am. Could have chewed on the leg of one of the outriders. But was not sure of my reception here so wanted to make it in good time to find an inn and hire a horse if necessary for the return journey."

"You thought I would cast you out of my home."

"Well, you have been treated abominably, Gabriel."

"Not by you, Godfrey. You always tried to affect the fashionable ennui, but you made a pretty poor job of it."

"I am an outcast in society. It is easier to pretend not to care, Gabriel. I am a bastard, after all."

"Some people may treat you with disdain, but you are the son and now the brother of a duke."

"They think I am like Cedric, and I am nothing like him."

Gabriel sighed. Now was not the time to undo years of sibling rivalry and Cedric's bullying ways. "We shall talk about it more when we get back to town. I can tell you for one thing—I am sure my duchess is relieved to see that you are wearing breeches rather than inexpressibles."

"Miss Violetta Masterson prefers me in these," he said grinning.

"You are wearing them for a young lady?"

"She is the granddaughter of the Earl of Moncliffe. His third son's daughter. She is five and twenty, and as pretty as a picture but she is lame. She needs to use a crutch to walk. Many in

334

the *Ton* have ignored her as a result. Her dowry is substantial. But I do not care about that. I am sure Father will have left enough for me. She understands me. I met her but a week ago, but I cannot wait until I see her again. She says she does not care that I am a bastard."

"She sounds delightful," said Gabriel.

"Yes, she does. People are idiots if they cannot see past her need to use a crutch. Why, we are friends with the Duchess of Kirkbourne and she uses crutches sometimes and is carried other times. She is delightful," put in Kathleen.

"So, if I marry a lame woman, you will not give her the cut direct?" he asked, hope filling his gaze.

"Never," said Gabriel, and Kathleen shook her head vehemently. Godfrey let out a breath and visibly relaxed. Damn, Gabriel hated society. The poor chit had a problem walking and had probably been ignored and insulted all her life.

"Maybe once we get back and everything is settled, we can have her around for dinner. And you as well of course," said Kathleen

"That would be kind of you. Thank you, Your Grace."

"Please, call me Kathleen, since you are my brother-in-law. So, when are we headed for London?" She turned to Gabriel. He glanced out of the window and grimaced.

"I thought mayhap we should wait until morning."

"I agree. Godfrey will be tired from travelling, you need time to come to terms with everything that has happened, and we would just be setting out when we would have to stop to rest for the night."

"I thought you said snow was not dangerous."

"Only freshly fallen snow. Look at the sky. It is clear. The snow shall freeze overnight and be like a frozen lake. The horses would break their necks. No, we should wait until morning."

"You really are like my own personal weathervane, my love."

"Only when it comes to snow. I know it better than you. Now I should go and speak to the staff about dinner and getting a room prepared for Godfrey. I shall be back presently."

Kathleen left, and Gabriel headed for the sideboard. Lifting a glass, he motioned to Godfrey who nodded eagerly. He really was a bit like a pup who just wanted to be loved. Gabriel was not sure he could manage to love his half-brother. Perhaps too much water had flowed under that particular bridge, but he could learn to respect the chap, given time. Now he just had to get used to the fact that the Duke of Hartsmere was no longer a man he despised. The Duke of Hartsmere was himself.

Chapter 22

"I cannot believe he left no will," wailed Lady Benwick into her handkerchief as Kathleen patted her hand.

Gabriel slid into the chair behind the desk in the Duke's study and looked around. Kathleen gave him an encouraging smile.

"I have consulted every solicitor my father ever had dealings with, his man of business and we have searched all his papers. There appears to be no will. As his eldest son, that means all properties and monies apparently come to me." He paused. He looked no happier about that news than the rest of the assembled group. His finances appear to be in good health.

"He has left my boys destitute. I am sure you are happy, Your Grace," wailed Lady Benwick. Kathleen's patience was wearing thin.

"Madam, you shall be quiet." Gabriel steepled his fingers and pursed his lips. Really it was poor form for the previous Duke to die without having left any kind of will. Kathleen and Gabriel had discussed it in bed the previous night as he had worried about what to do about it. She liked that he was willing to discuss business with her. "Let it be acknowledged that I am not my sire, and I am nothing like him. He may have refused to do his duty, but I shall not."

"Stalwood, did my father give you Christina's dowry?"

Stalwood stiffened. "No but ..."

"I shall give you ten thousand pounds as a dowry for her. Is that enough?" Stalwood's eyebrows rose.

"It is too much."

"Nothing is too much for my dear older sister," he said, grinning. Christina stuck her tongue out at him and Kathleen, Stalwood and Gabriel laughed. Everyone else just looked a little confused.

Gabriel looked at Lady Benwick. "Madam, I know you are well looked after by your late husband's estate. However, I have never doubted you cared for the eighth Duke. You bore him two sons, and you suffered much scandal to be with him. My feelings with regards to your part in my mother's death are neither here nor there. You shall receive three thousand pounds per annum until your death."

"My part in her death? You killed her."

"In what way did Gabriel kill her, Ma'am? He was a child? He did not know what he was witnessing. He thought the Duke was hurting you?" said Kathleen.

"Pardon? I have no clue what you are talking about, *Duchess*," Lady Benwick said, the contempt dripping off the honorific.

"My Lady, I was five. I was playing near the dower house, and I saw you and my father copulating."

"You did no such thing. I never ... not in his bed, not in his house and not on his estate. He always came to me."

"Even when you were married to Lord Benwick?" Gabriel raised a sceptical eyebrow.

"I was faithful to my husband. Much to your father's chagrin."

"But I saw him, smacking your arse and plunging into you. I thought he was beating you as he beat my mother. Of course, I knew not what sex was back then, and I thought you were a servant. I told my mother and the next night she killed herself."

Lady Benwick gasped. Her face was ashen, and she grasped for Kathleen's hand.

"She killed herself?"

"Of course. What did you think happened?"

"Well, your father just said you killed her. I did not ask for the details."

"So, was it you in the dower house that day?"

"I told you. I was never on your father's estate. Not even to visit my boys once he took them away from me."

"He took us away from you? He said you did not want us," said Godfrey.

"How could you think that? I loved you. I faced down scandal to have you," Lady Benwick protested.

"Were you having your affair with my father when I was five?" Gabriel asked, his tone strained.

Lady Benwick looked contemplative.

"I believe not. I think I may have been courting Lord Benwick at that point. Your father was furious."

"Good God. It is all coming out now," Gabriel breathed through clenched teeth.

"Perhaps mother did not kill herself. Perhaps he killed her." Everyone turned and looked at Christina. She shrugged. "They had an almighty row that night. He was bellowing, she was crying. He hit her a few times. I suppose we shall never know the truth. The reason I suggest it is that for many years there has been guilt and accusation and hatred in this family and I for one am sick and tired of it."

Christina crossed her arms. "The man who caused it all is dead. And thank God for that. He was violent and he was vile. It is time for us to move on. Mother was downtrodden and beaten by her husband. However she died, it was probably a blessed release. We now have our own blessed release from the same man. Let us not spend our time going over what might or might not have happened twenty years ago."

Everyone just stared at Christina for a few moments. Kathleen had to say something. She agreed with her completely.

"Yes, you are right Christina. It is time to move on. You were saying about money, Gabriel?"

Gabriel turned back to the notes he had written down. "Ah yes. Godfrey and Cedric, you shall each have three thousand per annum. However, Cedric, yours comes with conditions. You will get one thousand pounds every four months. If I hear any rumours or tales from servants, maids, or ladies that you have hurt them or forced them to do anything sexual or otherwise that they did not want to do, then you shall receive no more money."

"Excuse me, of what do you accuse my son?" Lady Benwick asked, straightening her spine.

"He abused my wife before he knew she was my wife and I have heard things from the maids." Gabriel said calmly.

"Is this true?" She looked at Kathleen.

"He asked me upstairs at the Arbuthnott soiree before Christmas but when I said no, he attempted to use force, taking me by the arm and dragging me away. The Duke of Kirkbourne intervened, and Cedric let go and I injured myself. Then he tried to force me again the night that Gabriel stepped in, and everyone found out about the charade he had been living."

Lady Benwick's gaze narrowed as her face whipped round towards her eldest son. "I see. Cedric, you and I shall be having words and you shall be mending your ways."

"But Mama ..."

"Do not 'Mama' me. You are a grown man. Is this how your father brought you up?"

"It probably was, Ma'am," said Gabriel.

"Mayhap," she said, visibly deflating. "He was a brute."

"Did he hit you, Lady Benwick?" asked Christina suddenly.

"Chrissie," Gabriel rebuked. She gave him an 'I only asked' look.

"Why do you think I stayed?" asked Lady Benwick. "Why do you think I came back only once my protector was gone?"

Kathleen took the woman's hand in both of hers.

"Gabriel is all the business concluded?" He nodded. "Then we shall all have tea in the drawing room. Lady Benwick, Cedric, Godfrey, you are of course invited along with Christina and Stalwood."

As they rose and Gabriel took her arm to lead her out, she smiled at him. He had started to mend the bridges with his family. They would work on the rest as time went by.

Chapter 23

December 31st, 1816

Please let us know when you hear from Sophia," Kathleen urged Lord and Lady Beattie as they stood at the door to see off their guests.

"I suspect she is in Cumberland. I have no idea if that is more or less safe, given the circumstances. But with all this snow, I doubt anyone would be stupid enough to follow her. I just hope she and the babe are well. It is a difficult enough journey in good weather."

"We shall pray for her safe return," said Gabriel, as he lifted Emily's gloved hand and pressed a quick kiss to it.

The butler opened the door and their friends walked out into the swirling snowstorm. Kathleen watched, slightly worried as her friend descended the steps. She was well propped up against her husband.

"Do you think the nephew of Sophia's husband really does want to kill her son?"

"People will do all sorts for wealth, power and money, my love."

"Men will. Not women."

"Mayhap. Well, my dear, our first large dinner as a married couple was perfect. Even our rather odd family of half-brothers, father's mistresses and Americans all got on quite well and Cedric behaved and wore proper breeches. Wonders shall never cease."

"I think Lady Benwick is ruling him with an iron rod these days," she giggled.

He escorted her upstairs and once their valet and maid had prepared them, Gabriel walked into her room. His face was drawn and pale and Kathleen held her arms out.

"Come, let us go to bed. You look exhausted."

"No, extinguish that candle and come and watch out this window with me."

She blew out the candle and found her way across the room. When she got there, he urged her to lift her sheer nightgown to her waist and straddle his lap.

"Your Grace, you are tired."

"Not so tired, I cannot bring in the New Year with my Duchess riding my prick," he said before he caught her nipple with his teeth through her nightgown. She gasped as the fingers of one of his hands probed her.

"Gabriel."

"Call me Your Grace. It arouses me."

"If you get any more aroused, *Your Grace*, that will not fit inside me."

He chuckled as she slid down onto him. His laughter turned into a groan of pleasure. Once she was fully seated, she took a moment to look out the window.

Large flakes of snow meandered down onto the street below. A solitary man walked around the square snuffing out the lamps. A town carriage made its way slowly down one side of Grosvenor Square. Candlelight could be seen in a few windows in the houses of the *ton.*

"What are you thinking about?" he asked as he started to move his hips and kiss her neck.

"Nothing. Is it not odd that less than a month ago we had not met?"

"A little but it does not take time to know you are in love."

"Hmm." She began to move with him still watching the snow fall. It was beautiful, just as their marriage was.

"Maybe this time next year the next Earl of Cindermaine will be in a crib in the nursery, or growing in your belly." He latched onto her nipple, and she dropped her head back to enjoy the sensation.

"Or maybe it will be Lady Elizabeth Marchby."

"Elizabeth? You like that name?"

"I do. Would you be terribly disappointed if we do not have a son first?"

"No. Maybe you shall have twins."

"Maybe. They do run in families."

"My mother had twin brothers."

"If not, we can have lots of babies until our nursery is full."

"I am not opposed to working on that, Duchess."

"Gabriel?"

"Hmm," he was kissing her neck again.

"Is that the church bells I hear?"

He stilled, and they both looked out the window and listened. "It is. They are chiming midnight. It is the Year of our Lord Eighteen Hundred and Seventeen. Happy New Year, my love."

"Happy New Year, Your Grace.

The End

To find out what has happened to Sophia, borrow or purchase Lord Rose-Reid and the Lost Lady at Amazon

You can also read book 1 in the series, Sleeping Lord Beattie on Kindle or Kindle Unlimited now

If you would like to read The Duke and Duchess of Kirkbourne's Story (Sarah and Nate) It can be found in A Desperate Wager

Click on this link to follow Em on Social Media

Follow this link to join Em's Newsletter

About the Author

Em was born and brought up in the Central Belt of Scotland and still lives there. She was told as a child she had an overactive imagination--as if that is a bad thing. She's traded her dreams of owning her own island, just like George in the Famous Five to hoping to meet her own Mr Darcy one day. But her imagination remains the same.

Printed in Great Britain
by Amazon